A STUDIO PRESS BOOK

First published in the UK in 2020 by Studio Press,
an imprint of Bonnier Books UK
4th Floor, Victoria House
Bloomsbury Square, London WC1B 4DA
Owned by Bonnier Books
Sveavägen 56, Stockholm, Sweden
www.bonnierbooks.co.uk

3 5 7 9 10 8 6 4

ISBN 978-1-78741-699-4 (Paperback)
ISBN 978-1-78741-952-0 (eBook)

MIX
Paper from
responsible sources
FSC® C018072
FSC
www.fsc.org

Written by Ned Hartley
Edited by Laura Pollard and Stephanie Milton
Cover illustration by Derek Charm

A CIP catalogue for this book is available
from the British Library
Printed and bound in the UK

**Ned Hartley**

AN ORIGIN STORY

# CHAPTER 1
# SPIDER-MAN
# IN SPACE

Spider-Man had never been more scared in his life.

Under the Spider-Man mask, Peter Parker grimaced. He was hanging onto the side of a space rocket as it hurtled upwards. He was gripping on with all his might, but it felt like he was about to be pulled off the rocket at any moment and thrown back towards the ground. His Spider-Man costume felt cold against his skin.

As the rocket climbed higher and higher, he looked back down. This was a mistake. He had no way of telling exactly how far he was from the ground, but it was very, very high up.

'Hey, I can see home from here!' he said. It was true. As well as the skyscrapers of Manhattan, he could see all the way to the small suburb of Forest Hills in Queens, where he lived.

'How did you get yourself into this one, Spidey?' he asked himself.

It had all happened so quickly. Peter Parker had been on a high-school trip to see the launch of experimental space shuttle, *Osborn-6*. However, within seconds of the shuttle taking off, it was obvious that something was wrong. The shuttle was moving too slowly and alarms were sounding all around the viewing station.

Peter had raced away from the rest of his class to change into his Spider-Man costume. He was already wearing the full red-and-blue bodysuit, with a spider logo on the front, under his school clothes. Peter had quickly put on the Spider-Man gloves and boots that were hidden in his backpack. The Spider-Man mask had gone on last; this was the part that made him feel like he had really changed – like he had become someone completely different.

As Spider-Man, he had rushed to the Oscorp launch pad and talked to the ground-control staff. Together they had persuaded the pilot of a light jet plane to fly him close enough to jump onto *Osborn-6*.

Now he was clinging on to the side of the space shuttle for dear life.

'Spider-Man! Can you hear me?' crackled a voice in his ear.

'Yes, of course I can!' said Spider-Man, before he remembered who he was talking to. He had been given an earpiece before he took off, and he was talking to Mission Control.

'You need to find a way to separate the rocket from the capsule with the astronauts,' said the voice in his ear.

'Sure, that sounds fine,' said Spider-Man.

'Should be easy. I mean, it's not exactly rocket science!'

Mission Control didn't reply.

Astronaut John Jameson III was aboard the shuttle, in a capsule connected to the rocket. John Jameson was the son of J. Jonah Jameson, the editor-in-chief of the *Daily Bugle* newspaper.

'Hey, could you do me a favour?' said Spider-Man to Mission Control. 'If there are any journalists from the *Daily Bugle* in the control room with you, could you ask them to write something nice about me? That would be cool!' He could do with some good press right now.

Spider-Man knew he shouldn't look down again. It was only going to make him more scared. The ground was too far away. He looked down again.

'Is this going to be more complicated than pulling out a bunch of wires?' he asked, trying to keep the fear out of his voice. 'Because otherwise all the movies I have seen have lied to me.'

'We're sure you can do this, Spider-Man,' said Mission Control, but the voice at the other end didn't sound too confident. 'Just move upwards to the big panel above you.'

Spidey was slowly inching his way up the rocket, trying not to think about how fast he was going or how it was becoming harder to breathe.

'I think I've found the right panel,' he told Mission Control. 'Hey! There's a red wire and a blue wire! I'm pulling the red one.'

*BOOM!*

The main capsule flew away from the rocket, just like it was supposed to. Spider-Man smiled under his mask as he held onto the falling capsule. A feeling of relief spread from the tip of his forehead, down through the rest of his body. He had done it. Spider-Man had saved the day!

Any moment now the parachute in the capsule would open and they would all glide gently to the Earth. Any moment now...

The parachute wasn't opening.

Now, instead of rising too quickly, he was falling too quickly. He was going to have to do something. Fast.

'Hello? Scientist guys in my ear? The parachute in the capsule isn't working! Any idea how I get it open again?' he asked, but there was no response. The earpiece had lost its connection to Mission Control.

For a second, he froze. What did he, a teenager from Queens, think he was doing, trying to save a space shuttle? And now it was all going wrong and it was entirely his fault!

What was he going to do?

Spider-Man spent a few seconds banging on the side of the capsule. He was trying to release the parachute, but also it made him feel better. If only he was a real spider, he thought to himself. Then he could just float away.

Wait a minute... maybe spiders were the answer! Some spiders used their threads to float through the wind on air currents. He remembered watching a documentary about it with his Uncle Ben. It was called 'ballooning', and it happened when spiders spun triangular parachutes to catch the wind. Maybe he could do the same!

Working faster than he ever could have thought possible, Spider-Man started to create a large triangular net, using the mechanical web-shooters in his wrists. As he spun and spun, a makeshift parachute started to take shape.

It was working! Although there were holes in the net, it was slowing the descent of the astronauts' capsule, and he could use it to steer the capsule towards the East River, which separated Manhattan and Queens. The most important thing was to make sure the capsule didn't crash anywhere where it could hurt a lot of people.

The capsule was still falling at speed, and Spider-Man was not at all confident that this would work. But it had to. Everything was moving towards him quickly and—

With a massive *FWOOOSH*, the capsule landed in the river in a huge explosion of sound and water.

Spider-Man was thrown up in the air, then pulled under the water. He was spun around under the current so many times he didn't know which way was up. He kicked out, trying to push himself through the water. Then he surfaced, coughing and spluttering in the East River. He could see the capsule opening – the astronauts looked a little shaken, but they were safe.

Spider-Man looked up and saw a giant electronic screen advertising the *Daily Bugle* newspaper, with the words *SPIDER-MAN – MENACE!* staring down at him. J. Jonah Jameson had never liked Spider-Man. Even though Spidey had just saved his son, Jonah wasn't going to say anything nice about him. In fact, it looked like he hated Spider-Man even more now, for upstaging his son's big event.

Spider-Man sighed and started to swim to shore.

## CHAPTER 2
# THE DAY EVERYTHING CHANGED

To understand Spider-Man, you need to understand Peter Parker.

Petcr Parker was born in Queens, which is in New York state, just next to the island of Manhattan. Until the age of six, he was brought up by his parents, Richard and Mary Parker.

Everything changed when Peter was six years old. He had finished his day at elementary school, but his mother was not there to pick him up. His uncle Ben was waiting for him instead.

Uncle Ben was a round, smiling man with

brown hair. Peter loved him, but he didn't understand why his mother wasn't there. Uncle Ben talked to Peter's teacher and then bent down to talk to Peter.

'Peter, I'm here to collect you from school today,' he said.

Uncle Ben walked Peter to his car. They both waited while Peter's Aunt May got out of the car. She hugged Peter a little too hard. Aunt May had her long hair in a bun, and it looked like she had been crying.

'Something has...' began Uncle Ben. Then he stopped. 'You're going to come live with me and your Aunt May. Something happened to your parents. There was a plane crash. I'm so sorry, Petey.'

His aunt hugged him again and started crying.

From that moment on, life was different.

Uncle Ben and Aunt May's house was smaller than Peter's old house and it was in a different part of Queens. The first few months were the hardest for Peter. He screamed and shouted, demanding that his parents take him home. When would they be back to pick him up? Aunt May and Uncle Ben were always kind and patient, they did everything they could to make Peter feel at home. Peter had his own room and as many science books as he could read, but at first he was inconsolable.

As time went by, Peter started to adjust to his new life. Peter, May and Ben liked watching nature documentaries together, then making lists of their favourite animals and insects. Once, Aunt May took Peter to the zoo and he spent the whole of the next day drawing pictures of all the animals he could remember.

One day after school, Peter's friend Ben asked him, 'Do you have a science project this year?'

'Yeah – I get to choose my own project this year,' said Peter. 'I was thinking it would be cool to find a way to trap animals without hurting them.' There were mice living in

Uncle Ben and Aunt May's house, but Peter would never let them use animal traps that killed them.

'How would you do that?' asked Ben.

'I don't know, some kind of glue that dissolved in the morning?' said Peter. 'That way you could catch the mouse... uh... animal, but then let it go later.'

Peter and Ben spent the afternoon making different types of glues and adhesives, but none was quite right. The boys ended up gluing several plates to the living room table, which they both thought was funny. In the end they agreed to come back to it another day.

Over the next few years, Peter and Ben worked on more and more science experiments together. Peter loved inventing things with Ben and he stopped missing his parents quite so much. Soon, Peter was sharing everything with Aunt May and Uncle Ben. They were the most important people in his life.

Ben and May didn't have much money, but
they did everything they could to make sure
that Peter was as happy as possible. When
Peter turned ten, his aunt and uncle took
him to see his first wrestling match, at a local
gym. Peter had watched hundreds of matches
on TV. His hero, Crusher Hogan, was in
town and he was very excited to go.

The moment Peter walked in, he could
hear the crowd chanting 'CRU-SHER!
CRU-SHER! CRU-SHER!' He couldn't
stop smiling.

Uncle Ben noticed how happy he was
and hugged him tight. Aunt May usually
disapproved of Peter watching wrestling
on TV, but now she was smiling back at
Peter, pleased to see him enjoying himself.
Peter suspected that May secretly enjoyed
watching wrestling too, as she knew all the
wrestlers' names and chanted along with the
rest of the crowd.

The main event was Crusher Hogan
fighting the Masked Wrestler. Peter didn't

know the Masked Wrestler, but he liked the air of mystery around him. Crusher fought the Masked Wrestler valiantly, but the masked man was stronger than him, knocking him down time and time again.

'Crusher is going to lose!' said a worried Peter, turning to Uncle Ben.

Uncle Ben didn't say anything. He smiled and pointed to Crusher Hogan, who was climbing back into the ring after being thrown out for the second time. There was something different about Crusher now, he had a look of determination on his face. The Masked Wrestler raised his arm, bringing it down to strike Crusher...

... and Crusher caught the blow!

He held the Masked Wrestler's wrist, while raining down punches with his free hand. Then, while the Masked Wrestler was stunned, Crusher lifted him up above his head and threw him down on the ground!

*BAM!* The sound of the large man hitting the canvas floor was deafening! Crusher quickly pinned him, holding his opponent against the floor for the count of three, to win the match.

On the way home, Peter talked excitedly about how Crusher Hogan had nearly lost the match, but had come back to win.

'He never gave up,' said Uncle Ben. 'Even when it looked like all was lost. That's an important life lesson, Peter. Never give up.'

As they walked in the door, Peter realised that he couldn't imagine his life without Uncle Ben and Aunt May now. He was very happy.

Peter, Ben and May went to see Crusher Hogan every year after that.

# CHAPTER 3
# MIDTOWN HIGH SCHOOL

Six years later, Peter was still a fan of
Crusher Hogan. By now Peter was a thin
sixteen-year-old teenager at Midtown High
School. He had short brown hair and wore
glasses. Peter didn't know much about
fashion and tended to wear simple outfits
like white shirts with loose jeans.

He loved science and spent more time in
the school labs than with his classmates.
Uncle Ben had encouraged him to read
science books and conduct his own
experiments, and Peter had proved that he
was a natural scientist.

But Peter found it hard to talk to people his own age. Teachers liked him, but he usually sat alone at lunchtime. He sometimes wondered what he would do if he had lots of friends. He still shared almost every part of his life with Uncle Ben and Aunt May, but it would have been nice to have someone his own age to talk to.

On the Friday before the annual wrestling match, Peter was late for school. He had been reading a book about particle physics and lost track of time, but he really didn't want to be late for science class. Unfortunately, Flash Thompson spotted him in the corridor.

'Where are you going, Parker?' yelled Flash, stepping in close so he was shouting in Peter's face.

Flash was a tall teenager who seemed to have a permanent sneer. He had a shock of slightly-too-long blond hair that he was constantly brushing out of his eyes. Flash was the star of the school football team, which he thought made him the most important person in the school. He was definitely popular; he always had a group of friends clustered around him, laughing at his jokes.

Peter was already worried because he was late for class. He tried to slip past Flash without making eye contact, but it was impossible. Flash was a bully and had a talent for choosing the worst possible moment to pick on people.

'What's the rush?' Flash asked, pushing himself close to Peter. 'You got a date with a science book?' The three other football players who always hung around with Flash seemed to find this hilarious.

'Maybe *you* should try dating one. I've seen your test results.' Peter tried to smile in a confident way as he said this, but he knew that he just looked nervous.

*WHAM!*

Flash punched Peter's locker, denting it and breaking one of the hinges. Peter looked around for help, but everyone else was in class. He could really do with a friend right about now.

'You think you're so smart, bookworm?' said Flash.

'Why? Are you looking for a tutor?' quipped Peter, then immediately regretted it. Why couldn't he stop himself saying things like that? Why did he always have to act like he was the smartest guy in the room? This was why he didn't have any friends!

Flash grabbed Peter, pulling him close and ripping the collar of Peter's shirt. Peter closed his eyes.

Before Flash could do anything, the school bell rang, signalling the start of class. The corridors of Midtown High started to empty as students ran to their first class.

Flash stood still, not letting go of Peter.

'Uh, Flash?' said Peter. 'Don't know if you knew this, but that bell means it's the start of class. You know, classes that we should be going to?'

Flash didn't move. He still had a lopsided smirk on his face. Peter realised what Flash was doing. If Flash punched Peter he would get in trouble, but if he just held Peter there then they would both be late and both get in trouble.

'Flash, we're going to be late. Come on!'

Peter was getting upset now. He didn't want to be late, especially not for science class. Science class was his favourite thing about Midtown High, and now Flash was taking it away from him. If he didn't get to class soon then he would be sent to the Principal and would miss the whole lesson.

'Just let me go!' said Peter, wriggling and trying to break loose from Flash's grip. Peter's collar ripped a little more. He didn't have many shirts, so he would have to ask Aunt May to fix it when he got home. She wasn't going to be pleased.

Peter and Flash were the only two people left in the corridor. Even the other football players had disappeared. Peter could feel the tears welling up behind his eyes, but he wasn't going to cry, not in front of Flash. That would mean that Flash had won.

But Peter was getting desperate. Mr Warren, the science teacher, would have noticed that he wasn't in class by now. He was going to get in trouble.

Then Peter heard a voice down the hall.

'Flash Thompson! What are you doing?'

Peter turned and saw Liz Allan, the prettiest girl in his class, storming towards them with an angry look on her face.

Flash let go and Peter slumped to the floor. His shirt was ripped and he was late for class, but at least Flash wasn't holding him any more. Peter wondered for a moment whether to thank Liz, but when he opened his mouth, no words came out. Instead he just stared at her with his mouth hanging open, a blank expression on his face.

'Aw, we were just messing around, weren't we, Parker?' said Flash. There was something in Flash's smile that said *You'd better agree with me, or else,* so Peter nodded.

Peter tried to stand up, but he was so flustered he tripped over his own legs and fell to the floor again.

Flash found this hilarious. 'Look at the bookworm!' he laughed. 'Maybe you should read some books about how to stand up properly!' This wasn't a great insult, but Peter couldn't think of a decent reply, so he didn't say anything.

'Peter Parker, what is the matter with you? You're so strange sometimes!' said Liz. 'Come on, you two. Let's get to class!'

Two minutes later, Liz breezed into the science classroom, waving airily at Mr Warren.

'Sorry we're late,' she said. 'We were working on the yearbook.'

Flash grinned and nodded, while Peter turned very pale indeed. He held his breath, wondering if they were going to get away with this, but Mr Warren just nodded and waved them towards three empty seats near the back of the class.

Peter sat down and Liz sat beside him with a wink. She had just saved him from Flash and managed to get him out of trouble with Mr Warren too. Maybe today was his lucky day...

'Liz,' he whispered. 'Are you busy tonight? Would you like to come to a science exhibition? It's about radiation!'

'Oh Peter,' laughed Liz. 'I'm going to Sally's party tonight with Flash. Science exhibition? You're so weird!'

# CHAPTER 4
# THE
# SPIDER

The rest of science class passed quickly. Peter found it hard to pay attention with Liz beside him, even though he usually loved science.

After school, Peter started walking straight to the science exhibition on his own. He hadn't been invited to Sally's party, and although he pretended that he didn't care, it was hard not to. He wondered what the party would be like. He'd never been to a teenage party before – he'd only seen them on TV and in movies.

The science exhibition was being held

at Oscorp Industries, which was three blocks from Midtown High. Peter hoped that someone else his own age would be there. Maybe he would make a new friend – someone who he could talk to about science. Perhaps another teenager who also found it hard to fit in at school...

The science exhibition was nearly deserted, and the few people who were there were much older than him. A tall, middle-aged woman was talking to a white-haired man with a cane.

Peter sighed to himself. So much for making new friends his own age.

The Oscorp Industries laboratories were based in an old building with stone pillars and high ceilings. They didn't look like the cutting edge of scientific research, thought Peter, they looked like they were part of an old horror film. A large banner saying *EXPERIMENTS IN RADIOACTIVITY* fluttered by the door, along with a smaller sign saying *OPEN TO THE PUBLIC*.

Despite everything, Peter smiled. He had been looking forward to this demonstration all day, and he was interested to see how the scientists at Oscorp had come up with new ways of measuring radioactive decay. No one else in his class seemed interested in this sort of thing, but it fascinated him.

High above Peter Parker, a lone spider started to lower itself from its web. The spider had been living in the laboratory for the last week but it was so high up that nobody had noticed it. It was about to change Peter Parker's life for ever.

As the spider lowered itself closer and closer to Peter, a short man in a green lab coat walked out in front of the small crowd and began the demonstration.

'Is this... Is that everyone?' asked the man. He peered at the crowd through thick wraparound glasses. 'Pitiful. Well, I suppose this will have to do. My name is Doctor Otto Octavius. I expect you have all heard of me. My demonstration today is about my revolutionary new theory for perpetual energy!'

Peter had read an article about Doctor Octavius in the newspaper that morning. It had said Octavius was a brilliant scientist, but that he was quite difficult and demanding. Nobody else wanted to work with him, so he often ended up working alone. Peter felt sorry for Octavius.

'I will show you how we can study – and even reverse – radioactive decay, right here in the laboratory...' continued Doctor Octavius.

The spider above Peter's head was still descending on a thin, silky strand.

Octavius reached over to his laptop and typed in a command. Something above Peter's head started humming. Peter looked up to see a machine high above him that looked a little bit like the inside of a giant camera. The machine was giving off a faint yellow glow. The spider moved towards it to investigate.

If Peter had looked closer, he would've seen the spider above him touch the glowing yellow machine, then begin to glow itself. The spider had been blasted with a fantastic amount of radiation from the machine and had absorbed more radiation than any spider had ever absorbed before. Over the last week it had changed and mutated into something new. Now the spider was glowing yellow, and lowering itself towards the crowd from the glowing machine. But nobody saw it because they had turned their attention back to Doctor Otto Octavius.

Peter was fascinated by the demonstration. He was learning a lot about how radioactive particles decay, and how that could be used to measure timespans longer than the age of the universe.

'Of course, there are many dangers associated with radioactive materials,' Doctor Octavius was saying. Peter was at the back of the crowd, and he leaned forwards to listen.

A moment later, the glowing spider landed

on Peter's head. He didn't notice. Weakly, the radioactive spider started to crawl across Peter's head. It slowly scuttled down his hair and onto his collar. Peter didn't feel a thing.

The spider reached Peter's right shoulder and began to climb down his right arm. Peter was so engrossed in the talk that he still didn't notice. The spider's long legs carried it all the way down Peter's arm.

The spider paused when it reached Peter's hand. It had no way of knowing that it was full of radiation and might be dying. All it knew was that something was very, very wrong and it had to do something.

The radioactive spider bit Peter Parker's hand.

'YEOOWWW!' screamed Peter, and everyone at the demonstration turned to look at him. Doctor Octavius stopped mid-sentence and cleared his throat.

'A-hem! Young man,' said Octavius. 'I understand that this demonstration is very exciting, but if you cannot control yourself, perhaps you'd better leave.'

Peter had more important things to worry about than Octavius. Something strange was happening to him. He looked down and saw that a spider had its fangs in his hand.

He swatted the spider away and it fell to the floor.

Peter wasn't sure what was wrong with him, but all of a sudden it felt like his bones were made of electricity. His head felt too far away from the rest of his body, like he was about to float away. He put out a hand to steady himself and nearly fell over.

'My head...' muttered Peter. 'I need some air...'

He fell over. Nobody helped him as he struggled back to his feet.

'Looks as though our experiment unnerved that poor young man!' laughed Octavius. But Peter was already running out the door.

## CHAPTER 5
# GREAT
# POWER

Peter didn't feel any better once he was out on the street.

Everything had changed, but he couldn't quite explain how. He was drenched in sweat, but he felt cold. His vision was blurry, his head was pounding and he wasn't sure, but it almost looked like his fingers were glowing.

That couldn't be right, could it? He was pretty sure that fingers couldn't glow. The spider bite on his hand was throbbing.

He felt as if his entire body had been charged with some sort of fantastic energy, but he didn't know how to get rid of it.

Peter was so preoccupied with these strange new feelings that he didn't notice that he had walked out into the middle of the road. He looked up and realised too late—

A yellow taxi was about to hit him!

In the last instant before the taxi hit, without even thinking about it, Peter jumped higher than he had ever jumped before.

For a split second, Peter was flipping and twisting in the air, like a leaf in the breeze. He didn't know how he did it, but he was safe. The taxi passed underneath him, and he landed on his feet.

'Stop daydreaming when you cross the street!' yelled the taxi driver as he sped away. Peter was too shocked to respond.

Peter ran all the way home. He was scared but excited at the same time. He wasn't sure what was happening to him, but he knew it was important.

When he got home, Aunt May and Uncle Ben were waiting for him. 'How was the science exhibition, Petey?' asked Uncle Ben. 'Did you make any scientific breakthroughs? Did you find a cure for the common cold?'

'I don't feel so good. I think I'm just going to go to bed,' said Peter, heading to his room.

'Don't you want anything to eat?' Aunt May called after him, but before she could finish her sentence she heard the sound of Peter's door closing.

Peter couldn't remember the last time he had felt this tired, not even when he'd stayed up all night one Christmas Eve, trying to pin a tracking device on Santa. He collapsed on his bed and fell into a deep sleep.

While he slept, his body changed. The huge blast of radiation had changed the spider, and now the DNA from the spider bite was mixing with Peter's DNA, transforming him into something that the world had never seen before.

When he woke up the next morning, he felt fine. Actually, he felt incredible! His headache was gone, his vision wasn't blurry any more... In fact, his vision was now so good that he didn't need the glasses that he had worn for the last ten years! He felt stronger, leaner and tougher.

'The new and improved Peter Parker 2.0!' he said to himself.

Just then Aunt May knocked on his bedroom door.

'Peter! You've been sleeping for ages,' she called. 'I know you're a teenager, but is everything OK?'

'Never better, Aunt May!' said Peter, bustling past her.

It was a Saturday, so he had all day to himself. The first thing he wanted to do was to see if he could repeat his huge jump from last night. He ran downstairs, and after grabbing a slice of toast for breakfast he was out of the house.

Peter lived in the Forest Hills neighbourhood of Queens in New York. It wasn't full of huge skyscrapers like the nearby island of Manhattan, but there were quiet side streets where he could try out his new abilities. He found a deserted alley behind a pizzeria.

It was a sunny summer day, and Peter looked around to make sure no one could see him. Finally, when he was sure that he was alone, he crouched down... and jumped as high as he could.

Peter flew high into the air, way higher than the two-storey restaurant. He felt like he was flying! This was AMAZING!

Before he knew it, though, he had reached the apex of the leap and he fell back to earth with a massive *CRASH!* He wasn't seriously hurt because a huge trash dumpster broke his fall. He climbed out of the trash. His jeans had a red stain down the left-hand side. He really hoped it was tomato soup.

Peter tried to jump again, but this time he put out a hand to touch the wall as he reached the peak of the jump. Somehow his hand stuck there, allowing him to cling to the side of the wall with the flat of his palm.

He slowly moved his other hand on the wall, and they both took his weight! By placing one hand then the other, he could use them to climb up the side of the wall! He was scaling the wall just as easily as he could walk.

This was spectacular! He had never seen anyone do anything like this.

Without even realising it, Peter was nearly at the top of the building. He looked around to see if anyone had noticed and saw a small child looking up at him.

He froze. The boy was about four or five. He had messy red hair and was wearing a black-and-white striped T-shirt.

As Peter looked down, the boy tugged at his mother's hand and said, 'Look at the man walking up the side of the building!'

Peter didn't know what to do! What if the mother saw him? How would he explain himself?

'That's the last time I let you read comic books, young man!' said the boy's mother, and pulled him away without even looking up in Peter's direction.

Peter breathed a sigh of relief and finished climbing up to the roof of the building. There was a steel pipe sticking up from the top of the roof and he reached out to grab it. It crumpled in his grip as if it were made of paper. He grabbed a brick and crushed it just as easily. Not only could he jump and climb walls, but he was also incredibly strong!

That wasn't all. Instead of climbing down to the ground, he found that he could gracefully walk along a steel cable, as if it were a spider's web.

Somehow the radioactive spider had transferred its spidey skills to him! But what was he going to do with these new powers?

# CHAPTER 6
## RETURN TO MIDTOWN HIGH

Peter decided not to tell Uncle Ben and Aunt May about his incredible new powers. He was used to sharing everything with them, but this was so strange, so out of the ordinary, that he didn't even know where to begin. Instead, Peter told himself that he needed to understand what was happening to him before he talked to anyone else about it.

He wanted to go to the Oscorp laboratories, but it was closed over the weekend. He would just have to wait until Monday before he could go back there to investigate.

On Monday morning, an upbeat Peter

Parker headed into Midtown High. He smiled at his classmates as he walked to class, waving to people he normally avoided and even stopping to help a girl carry her books.

'What's up with Parker?' he heard one student mutter.

'Just having a great day!' he yelled back.

Suddenly there was a pinching and an itching at the back of his neck. Something was wrong. He couldn't explain how he knew this, but something was about to hurt him.

In one quick and fluid movement he turned and raised his hand, catching the football that had been thrown at his head. The football had been moving fast and if Peter had been a split second later it would've hit him square in the face.

'Yo, Parker!' shouted Flash Thompson. 'So now you think you're good enough to make the football team?'

Flash was wearing his football jacket. He didn't apologise for throwing the ball or try to pretend it wasn't him. He just grabbed his football back from Peter and leaned in towards him.

'Stick to your books, egghead!' he whispered into his ear. Flash's friends, Carl and Seymour, laughed unkindly at Peter and jostled him as they walked past.

Normally Peter would've let it go. The old Peter Parker would've been grateful that he hadn't been hurt and just walked away. But today he felt different. He felt stronger, more powerful, more confident. He felt alive.

'What's the matter, Flash? Scared I'll beat you?' Peter replied. He felt strange, as if someone else had said the words.

Flash's hulking friends found this hilarious. Carl was bigger than Seymour and he put his hand on the other boy to steady himself, as if he was laughing so hard that he could barely keep himself upright.

'You gonna take that, Flash?' spluttered Carl through his laughter.

Flash had gone still and quiet.

Peter realised that everyone was looking at him. For the first time in his entire career at Midtown High, he was the centre of attention. Hadn't he always wanted to be noticed?

Suddenly Flash was running at him, holding the football close to his chest like the quarterback he was. He was yelling, 'You think you can stop me?', and he had a determined look in his eye.

Once again, Peter was jumping before he knew what he was doing. This time he judged it a little better, and he flipped gracefully in the air while Flash passed underneath him. Flash had kept his head down and crashed hard into the wall. He hadn't been wearing his helmet or pads and the collision looked like it hurt. Flash fell to the floor like a puppet.

Peter looked around. He recognised students from his other classes. There was Jessica from English class and Charlie from Maths. Everyone was looking at him like it was the first time they had really seen him.

He wished he could tell them about the spider bite. He wanted everyone to know that he was no longer the same old bookish Peter Parker that they whispered about behind his back. Something very important about him had changed. Maybe now they would invite him to their parties and include him on their message groups?

But Peter didn't say anything. He just turned and ran out of the school.

* * *

He was sitting behind the football pitch when Liz Allan found him later.

'Hi Pete,' she said, sitting down next to him. 'Mind if I sit here?'

It was turning into a very confusing day and he didn't know what to say. He always found it hard to talk to Liz. He was a little bit intimidated by how confident she was. He nodded at her without making eye contact.

'I heard about what happened with Flash, and I thought you could do with a friend,' she said.

Peter wasn't quite sure what to say, so he nodded again.

'You just have to stay out of his way, Peter,' said Liz. 'Just let Flash be Flash and don't let him get to you. Don't rile him up. It will only make things worse for you. You understand that, right?'

Peter shrugged. 'My Uncle Ben says that if you don't stand up to bullies then they just get worse and worse. He says that all bullies are cowards really.'

Liz sighed and stood up. 'Just think about what I said.'

'I don't want to hide from bullies,' said Peter. 'I shouldn't have to.'

'It's not hiding. Staying away from trouble is just being smart,' said Liz. 'You're smart, right?'

'I guess,' he replied. 'I just don't like running away.'

'Yeah, and I don't like seeing people being stupid,' said Liz. 'Flash isn't a bad guy. If you stay away from him then everything will be fine.'

As Liz walked away, Peter realised it had been the longest conversation they'd ever had.

# CHAPTER 7
# DOCTOR OTTO OCTAVIUS

After school, Peter decided to visit the Oscorp laboratories, the place where his life had been changed for ever. He had to find out more about what had happened to him. Why had a bite from a spider changed him so much?

As he walked there, he felt as if something important was about to happen to him. Peter didn't believe in destiny, but this felt special, as if he was meant to be there.

'Here we go, this is it!' Peter said to himself as he turned the corner and saw...

... the locked gates of Oscorp Industries.

Oscorp was an old building surrounded by a high wall, with large metal gates that were locked with a padlock and chain. Peter rattled the chain but the gate didn't open. He wasn't really sure what he was trying to do. The gates were locked.

He looked up. The wall was at least three times taller than him and had spikes along the top.

Deep down, Peter knew that he had to get into that laboratory. He needed answers. He needed to know what was happening to him.

He looked at the wall.

Then he jumped.

While he was soaring through the air, he felt spectacular, like this was who he was always meant to be.

He landed on the other side of the wall and scurried towards the main building. He couldn't see anybody inside so he walked up to the main doors. The doors unlocked mechanically and slid open automatically, but there was nobody at the main reception desk behind them.

Peter Parker walked into the Oscorp laboratories for the second time in his life. It felt different this time. It felt spooky.

'Hello?' he called. No one replied. The laboratory seemed deserted.

He walked further into the building. Perhaps there would be some clues for him inside. It was dark and creepy. Long shadows stretched in front of him.

'You must be the new intern,' said a voice very close to his ear. Peter jumped, startled, because he had thought he was alone.

Doctor Otto Octavius was standing next to him. When Peter saw him, he gasped, too shocked to speak.

Doctor Octavius was wearing a pale green jumpsuit and wraparound dark glasses that completely covered his eyes. That wasn't what was unusual about him, however. What was unusual was the metal harness he was wearing around his waist. It had four long metal tentacle-like tubes coming out of it, each with three-pronged pincers at the end. Each of these 'arms' was moving and wriggling, almost as if it had a mind of its own.

'I'm sorry that you wasted your trip, but I do not need an intern today,' Octavius was saying. 'As you can see, everyone else has gone home.'

Something felt wrong. There was a nagging feeling at the back of Peter's mind, that he was in danger right now. The metal arms started to wriggle towards him. One of them stopped and turned slightly to the side as if it was looking at him.

'What...?' asked Peter, pointing at the metal arms.

'Ah!' said Octavius, pleased with the attention that his harness was getting. 'Do you like them? I call them my arms!'

Octavius started to walk to the main laboratory then, and Peter followed him. Octavius was still talking.

'These arms are the reason I don't need

any other scientists. I am quite capable of doing everything by myself!'

One of the arms swung round, lurching dangerously close to Peter's face. 'They are very strong. Made of reinforced titanium steel, with telescoping rotation for 360-degree flexibility. Look, the pincers can fully rotate in their sockets.'

The pincers snapped near Peter's face, then retreated, writhing in the shadow. He felt uneasy.

'But how are you controlling them?' asked Peter. 'You don't seem to have a control console.'

One of the arms was starting to wind around his left foot now. It felt cold.

'Very clever!' said Octavius. 'I have built an artificial intelligence chip into each arm. They respond to my most subtle commands – a nod here, a flick of the eye there. They know what I want them to do before I do! Haha!'

Octavius seemed to find this idea very

funny indeed and paused for a moment to laugh at his own joke.

'Ha! Yes, indeed!' he continued. 'These arms allow me to perform the most dangerous and delicate of experiments without the need of any staff. I am the most brilliant atomic researcher in the country, and finally I can work alone.'

'But why don't you want to work with other people?' asked Peter.

'Because they are idiots!' snapped Octavius. 'None of them can keep up with my brilliance. And do you think I don't hear the names they call me behind my back? "Doctor Octopus"! They think they're so clever!'

Peter thought for a moment about the other students at Midtown High and the cruel names and the whispers he heard behind his back. Maybe Octavius was right. Maybe if you were a true genius you didn't need anyone else.

'I work with incredible levels of radiation

every day. I cannot afford to let people who aren't at my level make mistakes and ruin my work, maybe even kill me!' said Octavius.

The robot arms were circling behind Peter now. He felt desperately uneasy. All he wanted to do was get out of this place.

'I need to ask you a question,' Peter said, suddenly remembering why he had come to Oscorp in the first place. 'There was a science exhibition on Friday. Did you... Did you see a spider there?'

'A spider? Why would there be any spiders in my laboratory?' asked Ocatavius. 'No, I am sure there were no arachnids present.'

'What would happen if someone was exposed to these levels of radiation?' asked Peter, pointing to one of the large machines in Octavius's laboratory.

'Well, it wouldn't be good for them,' laughed Octavius. 'That's why I use these arms! Radiation is extremely dangerous. It can mutate your DNA, changing the cells that make up your body. In large doses it is deadly! The safest thing to do is to stay well away. Now, young man, you must leave,' said Octavius firmly. 'I have many important experiments and you have already taken up far too much of my time.'

Peter tried to look around the laboratories a bit more, but Octavius was ushering him out. He wasn't going to get any answers here.

On the walk home, Peter thought about Doctor Otto Octavius, alone in his laboratory with only his scientific equipment and his experiments to keep him company. It didn't sound too bad to Peter, especially when he thought about Flash Thompson and his other classmates.

# CHAPTER 8
# CRUSHER HOGAN

As soon as Peter got home he could tell
something was wrong. Uncle Ben was
waiting on a seat by the door, and he jumped
up before Peter had walked into the house.

'There you are!' said Ben, urgently.

Peter's mind raced. Was he in trouble?
Did Uncle Ben know about his new powers?
What was wrong?

'I was in the library... doing homework,'
said Peter. He hated to lie to Uncle Ben, but
he kept thinking about what Doctor Octavius
had said. Maybe it was better to go through
this alone.

'Uh-huh?' Ben didn't look like he believed Peter at all. 'Is that so?'

There was a pause. Peter wasn't sure what to say. Uncle Ben was joking, right? Ben was famously poker-faced and it was hard to tell with him sometimes.

'Well, come on!' said Aunt May, bustling past them. 'We're going to be late. And make sure you don't forget your coat!'

'My coat?' repeated Peter.

'Of course,' said Aunt May. 'We're going to the wrestling match tonight!'

It was their yearly trip to see Crusher Hogan. Uncle Ben and Aunt May didn't have much money and sometimes found it hard to pay the rent on the house. Peter knew that they had saved for months to get these tickets – and he had nearly missed the show!

The crowd was starting to gather as Peter, May and Ben arrived. A huge banner was hanging outside the gym, with Crusher Hogan's face on it and the words *WHO WILL THE CRUSHER CRUSH NEXT?* written underneath.

Crusher Hogan was already in the ring when the three of them entered the gym.

Peter had forgotten how big Crusher was! He was huge, perhaps the biggest man that Peter had ever seen. He was wearing a pair of purple shorts, and his bulging muscles and bald head made him look like an angry Greek god. Instead of waving and smiling, Crusher was shouting at the crowd.

'Who here thinks they got what it takes to take me on?' he was yelling. 'I look out here... I don't see anyone who could pin the Crusher!' He banged his chest to emphasise his point.

There was a sign next to the ring, saying *$3,000 TO ANYONE WHO CAN STAY IN THE RING WITH CRUSHER HOGAN FOR THREE MINUTES* in big letters.

'That's new,' said Peter, pointing at the sign.

'But who's going to get in the ring with that guy?' asked Uncle Ben, pointing at

Crusher Hogan.

Hogan saw Uncle Ben pointing at him, and pointed back. 'How about YOU?' yelled Crusher into a microphone. 'Come on, old man! Can you beat Crusher Hogan?'

Uncle Ben looked around him, then raised his hands and laughed. 'No thanks, Crusher! I think you'd crush me!'

The crowd laughed and Crusher looked to the other side of the ring.

A thought popped into the back of Peter's head. With his new powers, maybe he could fight Crusher...

Was he really strong enough to defeat a six-foot-six wrestler who had been fighting for almost his entire life? Peter was a bookish high-school student. This would never work... right?

May and Ben watched, confused, as Peter started walking towards the ring. He was going to challenge Crusher Hogan to a fight, he could feel it! His entire body was electrified. This was so exciting – he was really going to do it!

'Hey!' began Peter. And then someone pushed him out of the way.

It was Seymour, Flash Thompson's friend from Midtown High. Seymour O'Reilly was one of the biggest boys in the year – tall with messy brown hair and a scowl. Right now he was shoving his way to the front of the crowd and shouting out to Hogan.

'Hey, Crusher!' yelled Seymour. 'Three minutes in the ring with you and I get the money?'

'That's right, little man,' bellowed Crusher. 'Just sign the insurance forms that say it ain't my fault if I hurt you!'

Seymour climbed into the ring, then squared up against the wrestler. Seymour normally towered over everyone else, but he looked tiny compared to Crusher Hogan.

'You ready?' asked Crusher Hogan.

'Yeah, I'm gonna—' But the bell rang before he could finish his sentence.

*DING-DING-DING!*

Seymour moved to grab Crusher Hogan by the shoulders, but Hogan dipped down and slipped out of his grasp. Before Seymour could tell what was going on, the wrestler was grabbing his legs with one hand and his torso with the other.

Then, with one quick movement, Crusher Hogan was holding Seymour O'Reilly over his head.

Peter heard Crusher whisper, 'Go limp, kid, or this will hurt more,' and then the man threw Seymour to the ground.

*SLAM!* The crowd went wild.

As Crusher soaked up the applause, Seymour got back up to his feet and whirled around, trying to land a blow on Crusher. But once more Crusher was too quick for him. Crusher flipped Seymour's legs from under him, and the teenager was on the canvas.

'All you have to do is stay in the ring with me for three minutes, kid!' said Crusher as Seymour got up again. Seymour didn't look as if he was enjoying this at all. He screwed up his face, took in a deep breath, then ran straight for Crusher as hard and fast as he could.

Which made it all the easier for Crusher Hogan to move out of the way and send Seymour flying out of the ring and into the crowd.

'Sorry! No money for you!' taunted Crusher.

Uncle Ben and Aunt May helped Seymour to his feet. He thanked them and walked unsteadily away.

'That boy goes to your school,' said Aunt May. 'You would never be so reckless as to go into the wrestling ring like that, would you, Peter?'

Peter shook his head. 'No, Aunt May,' he said.

Uncle Ben looked sad. 'It wasn't right what Crusher Hogan did,' he said. 'He's more powerful than that kid. With great power comes great responsibility.'

But Peter wasn't really listening. He was thinking about how he could get in that ring without anyone knowing it was him.

# CHAPTER 9
# THE AMAZING
# SPIDER-MAN

Peter Parker had a plan. He was going to use
his powers to win that $3,000 and give it
to Aunt May and Uncle Ben. He knew they
were behind on the rent to their landlord and
they needed the money.

After seeing the way Aunt May and Uncle
Ben had looked at Seymour O'Reilly, Peter
knew he would have to disguise himself.
He didn't want to look ridiculous in front of
everyone.

Peter had watched enough wrestling
matches to know that he needed something
to catch the crowd's attention. As soon as

he got home after the wrestling match, he
emptied his closet, looking for anything
he could use as a costume. T-shirts, vests,
hoodies and shirts all flew onto his bed.

What should his wrestling name be? What
made him different from everyone else? He
thought back to the spider bite that gave him
his powers. That was it! He would be...

... the Human Spider!

No. That was awful.

The Spiderator? Kid Spider? Captain
Arachnid? The Arthropod?

Perhaps he should choose the costume
first, then maybe a name would come to him
later. He chose a white, long-sleeved T-shirt
and with a black pen he carefully drew a
picture of a spider on it. He looked at himself
in the mirror. He looked pretty cool, but his
face was still visible. He solved that problem
by borrowing a black netted scarf from Aunt
May and winding it around his face.

Perfect! The scarf hid his face, and looked
a little like a spider web, which would add to

the theme.

If he was quick, he might still be able to get back to the gym in time for the second show of the night and challenge Crusher Hogan.

Peter carefully opened his bedroom window and climbed down, sticking to the wall as if gravity was no longer a factor.

When he arrived at the gym, the mood seemed different. The crowd had turned sour and it felt as if they were getting tired of being insulted by Crusher Hogan.

'Which of you no good, lily-livered, cowardly—' Crusher was shouting.

'I'll try for that money, Crusher,' said Peter, cutting him off because it didn't sound as if Crusher was ever going to finish.

Peter put his hands on his hips and tried to look brave in front of the crowd. In the bright lights of the gym his costume didn't look quite so good any more. He felt very, very nervous. What if he failed? What if Crusher made him look like a fool? What if his mask came off and everyone saw who he was and laughed at him at school the next day?

'Well, well, well,' yelled Crusher, waving his arms around and hamming it up for the crowd. 'If it ain't a little masked marvel!'

Peter walked up to the edge of the ring. With every step, he was less sure that this was a good idea. He noticed that his legs were shaking a little.

Crusher waited at the other side of the ring as Peter climbed in. He was grinning and pointing at him.

'Now, just relax,' growled Crusher. 'I'll try to make this as painless as possible!'

This got a big laugh from the crowd.

Before Peter knew what was happening, Crusher was running for him, arms outstretched, ready to grab him. Crusher's arms were huge, as big as tree trunks, and he could do a lot of damage to Peter.

But Peter leapfrogged over the surprised Crusher Hogan. The crowd roared!

Crusher's face was a picture of surprise, but he was obviously determined not to be beaten by such a small opponent. He whirled around, trying to catch Peter with his huge fist.

Again, Peter was too fast. He wasn't even thinking about it; he had a new sense that he couldn't describe. It was a spider-sense – his body was reacting to the threat as if it was second nature. He could feel something tingling at the back of his neck when Crusher tried to grab him.

Crusher tried again and again to strike Peter, but the teenager was slightly ahead of him, always anticipating his next move.

Peter could hear people cheering for him, and he looked out into the crowd and waved. He had never heard people cheering for him before, and he liked the feeling. He liked the cheering so much that he stopped concentrating on what Crusher was doing. This was a big mistake.

While Peter was distracted, Crusher Hogan

used the opportunity to strike. Moving quickly, the wrestler grabbed Peter by the head, almost completely covering it in his giant fist.

Peter wriggled and wriggled, but he didn't have any leverage. He couldn't break free!

'You were fast, kid,' said Hogan. 'But sometimes that's just not enough!'

Crusher Hogan lifted his massive arm and threw Peter Parker out of the ring as hard as he could.

Just before he flew out, Peter grabbed the edge of the ropes and flipped himself back in. This was getting dangerous! He had to end this match quickly, before he got hurt.

Peter bent down, putting his shoulder towards Crusher Hogan, then reached round, grabbing the giant man. As quickly as he could, Peter lifted Crusher into the air as if he were as light as a child.

With Crusher now on Peter's shoulder, Peter bent his knees, braced... and jumped!

When Crusher looked down, he was high

above the ring! He didn't know how the boy was doing it, but Crusher's tiny opponent was holding on to the ceiling of the gym and dangling the massive wrestler as if he was made of paper.

'Put me down!' shrieked Crusher, covering his eyes. 'You win! YOU WIN!'

Peter gently returned Crusher to the ring, bringing him down with a condescending pat on the head.

'You... you're not human!' said Crusher. 'Nobody can do that!'

Peter didn't say anything. The crowd was cheering, and under his mask he was smiling so broadly that it nearly hurt his face. This was terrific!

The next few minutes were all a blur. Crusher weakly pointed Peter towards the back office of the gym, where a man in a blue tracksuit reluctantly gave him his money in cash. Peter walked back into the gym counting it, before realising that it wasn't a good idea to be waving that much money around. He put it in his pocket.

As he was walking towards the exit, a tall man with a purple suit, a bow tie and a short beard approached him. Peter had never seen anyone like him.

'Hi, I'm Maxwell Shiffman – a TV producer for *Late Night Live*,' he introduced himself. 'Your act is brilliant! I love the showmanship, the mystery of the masked man! I'd love to have you on the show! What's your name?'

Peter paused. What should he say? This name was going to define his new career. Suddenly, without thinking about it, a new name was on his lips. He knew what he wanted to be called.

'I'm Spider-Man,' said Peter Parker.

'I like it,' said Maxwell. 'But do me a favour, get a better costume, huh?'

Peter nodded. He was excited. He was going to be on television!

# CHAPTER 10
## THE ROBBERY

The next day, Peter gave nearly all the money he'd won to Aunt May and Uncle Ben. He didn't tell them about the wrestling match – instead he told them that he'd won it in a science competition.

Aunt May cried when he gave them the money. Uncle Ben clapped him on the shoulder and said: 'A good person takes responsibility for others and puts other people first. Well done.' Peter could tell that he was happy.

Peter had kept some of the money that he won from the wrestling to buy a new costume. He felt bad that he hadn't given everything to May and Ben, but he was really excited about being on television. He knew that he needed to wear something bright and eye-catching to impress the TV producer.

He went to the local sporting goods store and bought a blue bodysuit, along with a mask and gloves. He would be able to do all his incredible moves without his usual clothes getting in the way. It fitted him perfectly, but there was something missing. It didn't look quite right.

While Aunt May was out, Peter borrowed her sewing machine and some red fabric, and added red sections with black webbing all along the costume. He sewed the eye lenses from sporting goggles into the costume's mask to help him see. Then he added an image of a spider to the middle of the costume, so that the world would know he was Spider-Man!

There was still something missing. He needed to wow everyone, and at the moment he just looked like any other masked wrestler. He needed something else.

Peter stared out of his window. What would make him more like a spider? In the lower corner of the sill, he suddenly spied a spider web with a fly stuck in it. Of course – he needed webs!

He thought back to an old science project he had done with Uncle Ben. He had wanted to create something that could trap mice humanely, but the mixture he created was just too sticky. At the time he'd thought it had been a failure, but it was perfect now! All he had to do was recreate it.

Mr Warren, his science teacher, was happy to let Peter use the science room after class. 'It's a long-chain polymer... ' Peter had tried to explain, but Mr Warren had gone back to reading the news.

Once Peter had created a batch of the web mixture, he needed somewhere to keep it. If it was going to be part of his act then he would need to use it quickly. Shooting the webbing from his hands would be the easiest way to control it, so he created a wrist-mounted web-shooter for each hand, with a pressure pad in his palm to control it. All he had to do was tap the pad in his palm with his fingers and a jet of webbing would shoot out of his wrist. Easy.

Now he was ready for his audition at *Late Night Live*.

On the way to the TV studios, Peter was nervous. He'd practised several new moves, but he was glad that he had a mask to hide the anxious expression on his face. He was going to be performing in front of an audience, with bright lights and cameras.

'Kid! You made it!' said the producer he had met at the wrestling show, putting an arm around Peter and moving him in front of the cameras. 'You're late, really late! But I guess you don't need hair and make-up with a look like that, so we're OK. When can you start?'

'How about now?' said Spider-Man.

Spider-Man began by swinging out over the audience, then climbing up the wall and hanging from the ceiling. There were gasps and cries of 'I don't believe it!', followed by a large round of applause.

'What's the matter?' asked Spider-Man. 'Haven't you ever seen a friendly, neighbourhood Spider-Man before?'

For the next few minutes Spider-Man amazed the crowd. He used his webs to swing around the studio, flipping and turning in the air like a circus acrobat. He jumped great heights, lifted heavy objects and spun huge webs. He was a hit!

After his ten minutes were up, Spider-Man was ushered backstage by the producer. Peter felt important. He could see everyone looking at him in his red-and-blue costume, and he felt like a star.

Someone from the *Daily Bugle* newspaper wanted to take his photograph and Peter smiled for the camera before realising that no one could see his face under the mask.

The producer was talking very excitedly. 'OK, so we'll tape a pre-recorded section tomorrow daytime, then have you on *Late Night Live*...' he stopped for a second and stared at Spider-Man. 'How old are you, kid? Old enough to stay up late?'

'Yeah, I—' began Peter.

'You know what, don't tell me,' said the producer, as the two of them walked to his office. 'The less I know about who's under that mask, the less trouble I get in later on down the line. Wait here, I'm going to get your contract.'

The producer ducked into a nearby office, and Peter was left in the corridor on his own. As he waited, he wondered what he would say to Uncle Ben and Aunt May about where he had been that evening.

Suddenly there was a commotion at the other end of the corridor. A large, sweaty security guard was shouting 'Stop him!' and a man with a blond beard and a scar was running towards Peter.

'If he makes it to the elevator, he'll get away!' yelled the security guard.

Peter realised that he was between the blond man and the elevator. What should he do? The man was obviously in trouble with the security guard, but it wasn't his problem. Spider-Man was a star – his job was to entertain the audience, not to capture bad guys. Somebody else could worry about it. This wasn't his responsibility.

Peter stood aside and let the blond man run past him.

'Thanks!' said the man, smiling at him before pushing the elevator button to shut the doors. By the time the security guard reached Peter, the elevator doors were shut and the man was long gone.

'Why didn't you stop him?' asked the exasperated security guard. 'What's wrong with you, kid? All you had to do was trip him up or hold him for a minute!'

'Sorry, pal!' said Spider-Man. 'That's your job, not mine.'

Peter thought about the man all the way home. Should he have stopped him? It really wasn't his job, but he could have helped the security guard. He only stopped thinking about it when he got to his street and saw police cars parked outside the house.

Something was wrong.

# CHAPTER 11
## GREAT RESPONSIBILITY

Peter ran into the house. A police officer had his hand on Aunt May's shoulder. She was crying.

'What happened?' asked Peter.

'Oh! Peter!' said Aunt May. 'It's Ben! There was a robbery. Someone tried to break into the house. Ben tried to stop him and... ' She started crying and hugged Peter.

Peter realised that there was an ambulance outside his house as well as all the police cars. He felt sick.

'Where's Uncle Ben?' he asked.

One of the police officers, an older man

with white hair, put his hand on Peter's shoulder. 'I'm sorry,' he said. 'The robber had a gun. Your uncle tried to stop him and...'

'He's dead, Peter,' finished Aunt May.

Peter felt the whole world fall away from underneath him.

'Where... is the robber?' is all that he could say.

'We're looking for him now,' said the police officer. 'We think he's in the old warehouse on the waterfront.'

Peter ran out of the house before he could hear any more. He had his Spider-Man costume on under his clothes, and he pulled the mask over his head.

The old warehouse was on the other side of town, but Spider-Man found that he could use the webs from his web-shooters to swing from the tops of buildings. He swung from building to building in long, looping arcs. He moved more and more quickly, determined to be faster than the wailing police cars below him.

Soon the empty warehouse loomed in front of him. It was a dark and shadowy building, the perfect place for a robber to hide.

Peter was scared, but he was also full of anger. All he could think about was the ambulance outside his house and poor Uncle Ben. He was going to make this man pay!

He carefully climbed up the side of the warehouse to the roof and entered the building through a broken skylight. He was making no noise, so that he could keep the element of surprise.

Spider-Man silently climbed across the ceiling, searching the warehouse. The killer had to be here somewhere.

Suddenly, he saw him! A stocky man in a leather jacket and green cap was crouched by a window with a gun in his hand. It had to be him. Peter edged his way towards the criminal, as quietly as he could.

*CRACK!*

Part of the ceiling was old and broken,

though, and it had split under his weight.
The killer turned quickly, pointing his gun at
Spider-Man. It was dark, and Peter couldn't
see the man's face.

'What the... ' said the criminal. He clearly
couldn't believe what he was seeing as
Spider-Man scuttled towards him across the
ceiling.

'Surprised to see me?' asked Spider-Man,
jumping down.

'Leave me alone!' shouted the killer,
backing away.

'You're not getting away that easily!' said
Spider-Man, leaping over him. Now Spider-
Man was blocking his route to the door. The
man would have to get past Spider-Man to
get out.

'No one can move that fast! I must be
seeing things,' muttered the criminal.

Spider-Man was about to reply, but he
suddenly felt the scratching at the back of
his neck that he had felt at school. It was his
spider-sense telling him he was in danger!

Just in time he saw the robber aim his gun. *BAM!* The first shot narrowly missed his right shoulder, and Spider-Man only just dodged out of the way.

*BAM!* The second shot also missed, hitting a part of the ceiling where Spider-Man had been only moments before.

This was getting too close, Spider-Man thought.

'There's no place on Earth where you can hide from me!' he shouted, trying to sound scary. Peter was still so angry that he found it hard to focus.

Then he had an idea. Maybe his webbing would be good for more than just swinging from buildings.

He fired his webbing at the criminal's right hand, completely covering the gun in sticky goo. He hoped that this would work.

The criminal aimed his web-covered gun at Spider-Man and...

Nothing. The gun was so gummed up it wouldn't even click.

'Not so tough without your little gun, are you?' said Spider-Man.

He launched himself at the killer, catching him hard on the jaw and knocking him to the ground. The criminal yelped, but didn't try to get back up.

When Peter bent down to pick the man up, he couldn't believe his eyes. The blond beard, the scar... It was the criminal from the TV studios earlier that day!

This was the man who had run past him. He could've stopped him. If he'd just been a little bit less self-obsessed, then Uncle Ben would be alive right now.

Uncle Ben's death was all his fault!

'No!' said Spider-Man, dropping the robber. 'Not you!'

If only he could go back and change time! Peter would've given anything to change the past, to stop the robber and save his uncle.

'Why?' asked Spider-Man. But he knew the answer. He had used his incredible powers to help only himself. He had been selfish and this was the result. With great powers came great responsibility, and he had ignored that responsibility.

There and then, Peter Parker made a promise to himself. From now on Spider-Man would use his powers to help and protect other people.

# CHAPTER 12
# WEB-
# SLINGING

The police arrived at the abandoned warehouse a few minutes later, but Spider-Man was already gone. The criminal was hanging from a long piece of webbing – slightly dazed from a punch on the chin, but apart from that he was unhurt.

When Peter got home it was late, and Aunt May was already in bed. He sat down in the living room and burst into tears.

The next few days were not easy. He kept expecting Uncle Ben to walk through the door at any minute. Or he would see something on television that would remind him of Uncle Ben. It made him sad when he realised he couldn't tell him about it.

School was hard, too. Everyone had heard what happened to his uncle, so they all felt sorry for him, which Peter hated. He could see it in their eyes – they pitied him. Being unknown was better than being pitied.

Two days after Uncle Ben died, Peter Parker was sitting alone in the lunch hall. He normally ate lunch alone, and he told himself that he didn't mind this. He was thinking about the next class after lunch when Liz Allan sat down next to him.

'Hey Peter, how's it going?' she asked.

'Hey Liz,' he said. 'I'm OK, I guess.'

'I heard about your uncle and I'm really sorry,' said Liz. She put her hand on his. The moment of warmth made Peter smile for a moment. 'Are you going to the school dance next week?' she asked.

Peter hadn't been planning on going to the dance – he didn't have a date to the dance, and he always felt awkward at events like that. Also, he didn't feel much like dancing right now.

'Why?' he said. Before he knew what he was saying he asked, 'Would you go with me?'

Liz laughed and looked away. But it wasn't an unkind laugh, it was something else. She didn't seem horrified at the idea of him asking her to the dance.

'Peter, are you asking me to the dance?' she said.

Peter had thought about it too much now and his sudden bravery had gone. 'I... er... Not if you don't want me to...' he spluttered.

'Well,' said Liz, getting up, 'if you're going to ask me then you have to ask me properly.' She walked away.

Peter had no idea what had just happened. Life was very, very confusing!

He decided that he needed to clear his head. Life might be complicated for Peter Parker, but it was easier for Spider-Man.

Without really knowing why he was doing

it, Peter had started wearing his Spider-Man costume under his clothes. It made him feel more in control: the secret of his dual identity gave him a feeling of power.

After school he waited to make sure that no one was watching him, then quickly climbed onto the roof of the school gym. His Spider-Man costume was already under his clothes so he was able to change quickly and put his school clothes in his backpack. Peter Parker had climbed up the building, but Spider-Man swung from the roof!

He practised using his webs to swing himself from building to building. He would launch himself forwards using the web to fling himself as far as possible and then letting go, spinning and twirling through the air. Then, just at the last moment, just at the point when he was about to go tumbling into the ground, he would fire another web and use that to propel himself forwards again.

Spider-Man was careful not to swing too close to anything dangerous, but he was moving so quickly that there were a couple of near misses. Thankfully the spider-sense in the back of his neck alerted him to danger when he was about to hit a truck or passing pedestrian.

The best place for web-slinging was right in the middle of New York City. That afternoon the huge buildings of Manhattan became his playground. Peter loved looking into the buildings of offices and seeing the shocked expressions of workers as he zoomed past.

As he swung through New York, he got more and more confident in his abilities. He came closer and closer to the ground with every loop, sometimes ducking in and out of traffic before catapulting himself back up in the air. It was exhilarating.

It got dark and started raining, but still Spider-Man didn't go home.

Spider-Man was swinging towards a stopped car with two young women in it, when he saw that they were waving at him.

'Hello,' he said. 'Yes, it really is Spider-Man from the television! Do you want a selfie or something?'

The women were pointing behind him and shouting something. He couldn't quite make out what they were trying to say to him.

'You'll have to speak one at a time,' he said, jumping on to the back of their car. Then he realised what they were shouting. They were shouting 'TRUCK!'. He turned and saw a huge, out-of-control truck zooming towards the small car. The car had stalled and wasn't moving, and it looked like the doors were stuck.

Everything seemed to slow down. He could see the truck barrelling towards him, far too fast to stop. The driver was slumped over the wheel. It looked like he was asleep or ill. There wasn't anyone else in the truck, and Spider-Man had to act quickly.

He jumped off the car and landed in the road, right between the truck and the car.

Spider-Man started shooting webs as

quickly as he could to create a net between two lampposts on either side of the road. He fired webs faster and faster, hoping that this would be enough.

The truck hit the webs and tore through them, barely slowing down. If only he'd had more time! If Spider-Man pushed the car out of the way then the truck would just hit someone else. He had to stop it. It was about to hit him!

'Well, here goes nothing,' he said.

Spider-Man braced himself, put his arms out, and took the full force of the truck. The impact sent vibrations up and down his body, but he steadied himself. The glass in the windscreen shattered, the bumper buckled, but Spider-Man did not move. Metal shifted and twisted all around him.

Then, everything stopped moving. He was alive! He had stopped the truck. He was battered and sore, and his costume was slightly ripped, but everyone was alive!

The women in the car were cheering for

him. 'Go Spider-Man!'

Spider-Man waited for an ambulance to arrive, to help the driver of the truck, then zipped away into the night. He had put someone else first; he had used his powers to help people. He felt good.

# CHAPTER 13
## AUNT MAY

Aunt May wouldn't admit that anything was wrong, but Peter knew that now Uncle Ben was gone, money was tighter than ever. They both missed Uncle Ben, but neither of them talked about it.

'I'll get a job,' Peter told Aunt May. 'I'm sixteen now, I can leave school and get a job to bring some money into the house.'

'Don't be silly,' Aunt May laughed. 'We'll be fine. And you need to keep studying so you can be a world-class scientist, remember?'

Peter felt guilty. He had spent a lot of

time being Spider-Man recently when he should've been studying. He was behind on all his homework, even science. He loved being Spider-Man so much that nothing else seemed important right now.

That evening, he used the family computer. Aunt May had left the browser open, and Peter saw that she had put a lot of her jewellery up for sale online. He knew that some of the jewellery had been in her family for years and meant a lot to her.

He needed money. Maybe if he couldn't make money as Peter Parker, he could make money as Spider-Man. He didn't want to do wrestling again. He hadn't enjoyed it, and it didn't look like Crusher Hogan could afford to lose another three thousand dollars.

Peter went to a payphone near school and called the TV producer from *Late Night Live*. He didn't use his own phone because he didn't want any links between himself and Spider-Man.

'Hi, this is... uh... Spider-Man,' he said

when the producer answered the phone. It felt weird saying it on the phone.

'Oh, hey kid,' said the producer. 'When are you going to come on the show? Everyone loves that whole spider thing you got going on!'

'Well, uh... that's the thing,' said Peter, trying to sound grown-up. 'I need compensation.' He had heard someone say that on television before.

'Compensation?' repeated the producer.

'Money,' said Peter. 'I want you to pay me!'

'OK, well you have your agent call me, and—'

'Uh, I don't have an agent,' interrupted Peter. 'I was thinking you could just, uh, you know, give me some money?' This had sounded less stupid in his head before he said it.

'Well, I can't really write a cheque to Spider-Man, can I, kid?' said the producer. 'How on earth are you going to go into a bank and cash it, eh? How will they know it's you and not just some kid in a costume?'

'Could you not just... give me cash?' asked Peter.

'Kid, what is the matter that you need money this badly?' asked the producer. 'Is this a gang thing?'

'I have to go,' said Peter and hung up.

He was feeling a bit down, so he decided to put on his Spider-Man costume and swing through Queens.

As he started to climb the side of the nearest building, he heard something in the distance. It sounded like police sirens. He climbed higher to get a better look.

Two police cars were chasing an armoured truck. The truck had obviously been stolen – he could see the driver had a mask over his face, and was trying to get away from the police.

Spider-Man looked down. He had to do something.

He used his webs to swing around, so that he was moving in the same direction as the police cars and the truck. The cars were driving fast, and Spider-Man had to swing quickly to catch up.

Soon he caught up with the truck and landed on the roof. The truck was swerving erratically from side to side, and it sideswiped one of the police cars, sending it crashing into the other one. It was up to Spider-Man to stop the truck.

He leaned down from the roof, sticking his head through the open window.

'Is this the cab I ordered?' he asked. 'Can you check the booking? First name "Spider", second name "Man"!'

The driver punched Spider-Man, nearly knocking him into the road.

'If you're not careful, then I'm going to start getting very angry!' said Spider-Man, dodging out of the way as the masked man tried to grab him. He jumped over the truck and stuck his head through the window on the other side.

'Are you driving this fast because you want

to get home to watch that baking show?' he said. 'It's pastry week, so I understand.'

The masked man tried to grab him, but Spider-Man dodged out of the way again.

'Careful! This costume rips easily!' he said.

This was getting dangerous. He needed to shut the situation down quickly. The only way to stop the truck safely was to climb in next to the driver. Spider-Man swung in through the window into the passenger side of the car, but the masked man was ready for him.

*WHAM!* The criminal punched him in the jaw, dazing him just long enough to get a second punch in. *WHAM!* Spider-Man's head was reeling and he couldn't focus.

'Ouch!' said Spider-Man. 'What did I ever do to you?'

Spider-Man leant back, brought up his legs and kicked the masked robber in the face.

The man went limp and Spider-Man reached over to gently steer the slowing truck to the side of the road.

That was when he looked behind him at the contents of the truck. It was FULL of money. Bags and bags of money, overflowing because they were so full.

Peter Parker stared. Any one of those bags of money would solve all Aunt May's debt problems. All he would have to do was lean back and grab one. No one would even notice that it had gone missing.

It would be so easy.

He thought about what his Uncle Ben had said, that good people take responsibility for themselves and look out for other people. He wanted to do the right thing. Uncle Ben might be gone, but Peter could keep his memory alive by living by his values.

Peter sighed. He did not reach back. He did not take any of the money.

Then he climbed out of the truck and waited for the police to appear in the distance, before swinging away.

# CHAPTER 14
# SPIDER-MAN: MENACE!

The next morning Peter saw a copy of the *Daily Bugle* newspaper on the kitchen table. There was a photograph of Spider-Man on the front page.

'Hey, cool,' he said to himself, thinking that he was finally famous. Then he picked up the paper and read the headline.

*SPIDER-MAN: MENACE!* was written in block capitals underneath his photo. There was a paragraph underneath it claiming that Spider-Man had been terrorising people all over New York, and that he had tried to steal the armoured truck full of money, before the police stopped him.

Peter was so angry he couldn't read any more. Why was the *Daily Bugle* being so mean about him? He had been trying to help people, and this was how he was treated? It was so unfair!

Aunt May saw him throwing down the newspaper and nodded.

'That awful Spider-Man,' she said. 'I hope they lock him up!'

Peter decided that he needed to improve Spider-Man's image. He spent the next week doing good deeds, so that the *Daily Bugle* would write positive things about him.

On Monday he saved a man from being hit by a train, pulling him out of the way just in time. The *Daily Bugle* called him a monster and said that he had caused the accident in the first place.

On Tuesday he stopped a mugging. *The Daily Bugle* wrote a story about how he probably had a real spider's head and that was why he wore the mask.

On Wednesday he stopped a space shuttle from crashing and saved the astronauts inside, including the son of J. Jonah Jameson, the *Daily Bugle*'s Editor-in-Chief. The *Daily Bugle* said he might be a shape-shifting alien, and he was the worst thing that had ever happened to New York.

On Thursday he realised that no matter what he did they were going to write horrible things about him. He decided to go to the *Daily Bugle* to find out why.

The *Daily Bugle* offices were in the Goodman building in downtown New York. It was a huge, forty-six-storey skyscraper made of shining metal and glass. Peter got out of the subway and stared up at the thirty-foot high letters saying *Daily Bugle* on the roof. Science was exciting, but this building was something different. This was where the news was made! He couldn't wait to be old enough to leave high school and work somewhere exciting like the *Daily Bugle*.

Peter took a lift to the thirtieth floor. He

knew that was where he would find the office of J. Jonah Jameson. Jameson had been writing awful things about Spider-Man. Maybe Peter could change his mind, if he could talk to him.

The *Daily Bugle* newsroom was a huge and noisy open-plan office, full of computers and people talking loudly. It was intoxicating just walking through it. Jonah had a small office at the edge of the newsroom.

A young woman was sitting outside J. Jonah Jameson's office. She had short brown hair in a bob and was wearing a black dress. She smiled at Peter as he walked towards her.

'Are you here about Spider-Man?' she asked him.

'Uh, yes...' said Peter, not quite sure how she knew.

Suddenly an ear-splitting yell came from the other side of the office door.

'MISS BRANT!' yelled a deep and raspy voice.

The young woman didn't take her eyes off

Peter. 'Don't worry about him. He's just a big sweetie really,' she said, nodding towards the door.

Peter gulped. He couldn't see into the office.

'MISS BRANT!!' the voice was louder now. Miss Brant didn't move.

'I'm Elizabeth Brant,' she said and held out her hand. 'Call me Betty.'

'Hi Betty, I'm Peter Parker,' said Peter, shaking her hand.

'MISS BRANT!!!!' This time J. Jonah Jameson stuck his head out of the office door. He was a wiry man with greying hair, a thick moustache and a scowl on his face. 'I've been yelling for you, Miss Brant!'

'Oh, I'm sorry,' said Miss Brant. 'I guess you forgot that talk we had about you not screaming my name across the office as if I'm a poodle.' She was completely calm while she said this, and smiled sweetly at Jameson afterwards.

Jameson stopped. He opened his mouth as

if he was going to say something, seemed to think better of it, then closed his mouth.

Instead, he pointed at Peter. 'Say, who's this kid?' he growled.

'This is Peter Parker,' said Betty Brant. 'He's here to sell you photos of Spider-Man.'

'Oh, no,' began Peter. 'That's not why—'

'Excellent!' said J. Jonah Jameson, putting his arm round Peter and leading him into the office.

'Spider-Man is a menace to this great city. Did you read my feature "Spider-Man is a Menace" in today's *Bugle*? Of course you did, that's why you're here! So, what photos have you got? And don't try to show me on any of those photoshop jobs. We can spot fake news a mile away!'

'I don't...' said Peter.

'Waiting to see the rates, are you?' snapped Jameson. 'Well, I can't blame you, in this economy. I'll give you a hundred dollars for every photo we use, and three... no... two-fifty if they're good enough to go on the front page. Someone's got to stop this masked maniac, right? I'm no hero, no matter what people call me. I'm just a concerned citizen doing my civic duty.'

Peter paused. Two hundred-and-fifty dollars was a lot of money. It would definitely mean that Aunt May wouldn't have to sell her jewellery. But the *Daily Bugle* was making Spider-Man look like a villain. If he gave them photos of himself, it might mean that people would hate Spider-Man even more.

'So... what you got?' asked Jameson.

Peter brought out his phone and carefully found a photo of himself as Spider-Man. He made sure that it didn't have a background or other features that could be used to identify him and it looked like someone else had been holding the phone..

'It's terrible,' said Jonah. 'I'll give you eighty bucks... fine. One hundred. But that's my final offer. Talk to Miss Brant and you'll get paid.'

On the way out Peter stopped at Betty Brant's desk.

'Hey Peter Parker,' she said, standing up and putting on her jacket. 'I'm finished for the day. Do you want to go get a coffee?'

Peter nodded.

As they were leaving they could hear Jonah shouting, 'And tell that kid to come back when he has more pictures of Spider-Man!'

Betty took Peter to a coffee shop across the road from the *Daily Bugle* offices. Now that he had sold a photo to the *Daily Bugle*, Peter was officially a photographer, and he felt part of an incredible new world. He felt like an adult.

Betty told him story after story about the bad-tempered J. Jonah Jameson, and he loved all of them. He realised that she wasn't much older than him.

'How do you get away with talking to Mr Jameson like that?' he asked.

'That's the thing about yelling at everyone about everything,' she said with a shrug.

'Sooner or later people just get used to you yelling and ignore you. I grew up with older brothers. You can't ever let men think they can get the upper hand. So, tell me about how you got those pictures of Spider-Man...'

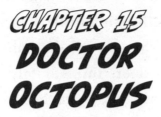

# CHAPTER 15
## DOCTOR OCTOPUS

Meanwhile, across town, things were not going well for Doctor Otto Octavius.

He had fired all his research assistants the week before, claiming that he didn't need them because of his superior robot arms. It was also partially because he had heard them laughing about him and calling him 'Doctor Octopus' behind his back, but he wouldn't admit that to anyone.

Otto had wanted to find a new energy source on his own because he didn't want to share the glory. He wanted people to adore him, but he didn't want to talk to them.

The problem was, now there was nobody around to help when things went wrong. He had been working non-stop for twenty-four hours when one of his arms knocked over a jar of radioactive chemicals. The automatic security measures in the laboratory had shuttered the doors immediately. It was late, and because Octavius had fired all the staff there was nobody else in the building. Doctor Otto Octavius was locked in.

Trapped and scared, he lashed out with the robot arms. Something exploded and he screamed in pain. There was a flash, and he knew that he had been exposed to something, but he didn't know what. He fainted.

However, the artificial-intelligence chips in his arms still worked, even when he was unconscious. His arms shot out, ripping the locked door of the laboratory off its hinges and smashing a window. They quickly carried the unconscious Octavius outside.

When Otto Octavius woke up a few hours

later, he was in hospital. A dark-haired nurse with a sympathetic face was standing over him.

'There was an accident,' began the nurse. 'Your mechanical arms... we can't remove them.'

'Let me up!' screamed Octavius. 'I must return to my work!' He looked down and saw that the metal control panel was still attached to his chest. He tried to move it, but it was permanently stuck to his body!

His metal arms were still attached to the control panel. They had been motionless, but now they sprang into life, thrashing around and smashing into the walls and the ceiling. The nurse ran for cover.

Octavius stood up, and his arms whizzed around him, helping him to stand. Something had snapped inside him. The pain and humiliation of his failure was too much for him to take. He was angry, but he couldn't bear to blame himself. It must be someone else's fault. Everyone else's fault!

As the medical staff ran from the room, Otto Octavius started laughing. 'From now on,' he shouted, 'you don't get to tell me what to do. NOBODY tells me what to do!'

Across town, Peter was finishing coffee with Betty when he looked up at the TV on the shop counter. There was a picture of Doctor Otto Octavius on the screen.

'Hey, I know him,' said Peter, as the picture of Octavius changed, showing him using his mechanical arms to smash a hole in the wall of the hospital. A banner along the bottom of the screen read *DOCTOR OCTOPUS GOES BESERK!*

'Do you think Jonah will want photographs of this?' he asked.

'Go!' said Betty, but Peter was already out the door.

A few minutes later, Spider-Man was crawling up the wall of the hospital. This is going to be easy, he thought to himself.

He could hear somebody shouting in a room on the fourth floor. When he peeked through the window, he saw that Octavius was holding two nurses hostage. Octavius was using two of his mechanical arms to hold them down, and seemed to be using his other arms to mix some strange-looking chemicals. Spider-Man carefully got out his phone and took some photographs.

'You have no right to keep us here!' one of the nurses was saying.

One of the metal arms grabbed her around the waist and lifted her up. 'I can do whatever I want!' said Octavius. 'And you would do well to treat me with some respect. I am your superior!'

'We can get you what you want,' said the other nurse.

Octavius was waving a piece of paper in the air. 'I *want* to go back to my laboratory,' he yelled. 'They sent me a letter, firing me. While I was in hospital! They did not even have the decency to tell me to my face! If Oscorp does not let me back into my laboratory then I will be forced to take drastic measures.'

That was all that Spider-Man needed to hear. If he waited any longer the nurses might get hurt, or worse. He jumped through the window.

'I guess it's true what they say about doctors making the worst patients!' said Spider-Man.

'Spider-Man!' gasped one of the nurses.

'Don't worry, folks!' said Spider-Man. 'Despite appearances, he's completely armless.'

'How dare you speak to me like that!' yelled Doctor Octopus, waving three of his arms at Spider-Man.

Spider-Man knew he had to keep Doctor Octopus distracted while the nurses escaped.

'I'm sure you wouldn't want the police to think you were *squid-napping* anyone, Doc,' he said.

'Shut up, you insignificant insect!' said Doctor Octopus, and two of the metal arms raced towards Spider-Man.

'You don't think those things are fast enough to catch me, do you?' said Spider-Man, jumping out of the way. He breathed a sigh of relief as the nurses ran out of the room.

While he was dodging two of the robot arms, a third caught Spider-Man by surprise, punching him in the face. 'Doctor Octopus is far more powerful than you imagined!' laughed Octavius.

'I'm glad to see you're reclaiming that nickname, but— *oof!*' Another arm caught Spider-Man in the stomach, making him lose his breath. This fight was far harder than he'd thought it would be.

There were too many arms for him to keep track of where they all were. Spider-Man fired his web-shooter, binding two of the arms together. 'That should hold you, squid-face!' said Spider-Man.

Spider-Man grabbed the remaining two arms with each of his hands. It took all of his strength and he could barely hold them.

They were superhumanly strong, maybe stronger than he was. Before he could do any more, Doctor Octopus snapped the webbing that was holding his other arms together. Spider-Man had never seen that happen before!

'I'm bored with this childishness,' said Octavius, grabbing Spider-Man by the arms and legs. Spider-Man was helpless. He wriggled and turned, but he was at the mercy of Doctor Octopus.

Octavius held Spider-Man upside down and stared at him, before lifting him slightly higher. 'Where are your brave words now?' Octavius asked. 'No funny comebacks? It's always people like you who stop people like me achieving brilliance.'

Spider-Man was stuck! No matter how hard he pulled with his super-strength, he couldn't escape. He felt exhausted, beaten and dejected.

'You're no threat to me,' said Doctor Octopus.

Then he threw Spider-Man through the wall of the hospital.

# CHAPTER 16
# THE TWO ELIZABETHS

Luckily for Spider-Man, there was a tree outside the hospital to break his fall. He crashed through the branches and landed on the ground.

He felt awful. His spider-powers had not been enough and Doctor Octopus had defeated him. He hadn't even been a serious threat to the evil scientist. At the end it had felt like Octavius had been toying with him.

Spider-Man saw Doctor Octopus leave the hospital, using his giant arms to carry him away. Peter picked himself up and began to make his way home. He was weak and hurt.

He was in no condition to chase Doc Ock.

The next morning, he left for school early so that Aunt May wouldn't see the bruises all over him.

Once again, Flash Thompson was waiting for Peter outside his classroom.

'Hey Flash, I'm flattered, but maybe you should focus your attention on someone else. I'm just not interested,' said Peter.

'You took photos of Spider-Man!' said Flash. 'I saw your name in the newspaper. How did you do it? Did you meet him?'

'You like Spider-Man?' asked Peter, incredulously.

'He's the best!' grinned Flash. 'He's not a bookworm like you, Parker.'

'Maybe you're right,' agreed Peter. 'I don't think those tights would suit me.'

Flash laughed at this, and for a second it looked like they might be friends. But then his expression hardened.

'But wait,' said Flash, grabbing Peter's shoulder. 'Why do you have to sell your photos to a rag like the *Daily Bugle*? All they ever do is print lies about Spidey! J. Jonah Jameson is the worst! Why does he have to be so mean about Spider-Man?'

'Oh, well... freedom of the press is very important, and—' began Peter.

'Nobody's going to fall for that!' yelled Flash in Peter's face. 'Everyone knows that Spidey is a real hero! So don't you sell any more photos to a paper that makes him look bad... or else!'

Flash stormed off, leaving Peter feeling very confused. Why was the person who liked Spider-Man the most in the world also the person who liked Peter Parker the least?

In science class, Liz Allan wanted to talk to him about Spider-Man too.

'Flash says you took pictures of Spider-Man?' she asked Peter.

Peter wasn't sure how to reply. He didn't want people to make too much of a connection between him and Spider-Man.

'Uh-huh,' he said.

'I don't like Spider-Man,' said Liz. 'He's dangerous. I know that Flash idolises him, but there's something... weird and creepy about him.'

'OK, I'll do my best to stay away from him,' he said. 'Flash really likes Spider-Man, huh?'

'He's pretty much a one-man Spider-Man fan club,' laughed Liz. 'Don't tell anyone, but I think that he might have a homemade Spider-Man costume hidden in his locker!'

Liz and Peter laughed so hard at this that Mr Warren made them stay behind after class. Peter had been getting lower and lower grades since he became Spider-Man, and now he was being told off after class. He still hadn't done last week's homework. This wasn't great.

Later, Peter emailed some more photos of Spider-Man to J. Jonah Jameson and asked him if he wanted to buy them. Jameson emailed him back to say they were boring and that he had seen pictures of Spider-Man like this before.

Another message from Jonah arrived in Peter's inbox a few minutes later. I need more exciting images of Spider-Man, it said. Peter decided to go to the *Daily Bugle* offices the next day.

Betty Brant was in J. Jonah Jameson's office when Peter got there. She was taking notes from Jonah, but Peter could see that her notepad was full of skull-and-crossbones doodles.

Jonah was mid-rant.

'... and call the Mayor to see if you can get him to say that Spider-Man is the worst criminal in the history of New York, or something like that. It has to be snappy. Worst Criminal Ever, or the worst thing to ever happen to this city. You let him decide, he'll know what to say...'

Betty waved at Peter as he entered, and Jonah immediately noticed this.

'Are you spending too much time with the photographers, Miss Brant?' he asked her.

'Well Jonah, someone has to be friendly to the freelancers before you scare them away with all your shouting,' replied Betty.

'Nonsense,' said Jonah. 'I get on just fine with Porter here.'

As Jameson was talking, Peter looked out of the office window. They were on the thirtieth floor and the view of New York was unforgettable.

Peter frowned and squinted at a shape in the sky. That looked just like Doctor Octopus, but it couldn't—

CRASH!

Two mechanical arms smashed through the window of Jameson's office. Jonah threw himself to the floor, and Peter moved in front of Betty to protect her. He was wearing his Spider-Man costume under his clothes, but he couldn't risk changing in front of everyone and giving away his secret identity.

Doctor Octopus used one of his mechanical arms to throw the desk across the room. It hit the far wall and splintered, sending wood and paper everywhere.

Next, Doctor Octopus pulled himself into the office. He used his robot arms to 'walk' across the room, while his real legs didn't touch the ground. This made it look like he was floating, which was very spooky indeed.

Jameson stood up. 'If you've got a problem with the *Daily Bugle*, then you talk to me,' he said. 'You don't need to bring these kids into it.' He gestured towards Peter and Betty. Peter was amazed that Jameson would be so brave.

Doctor Octopus looked him up and down. Then he laughed. 'Who on earth are you?' he said. 'I've come here for Betty Brant! She's Bennet Brant's sister.'

He scooped up Betty with one of his mechanical arms, wrapping it around her body. Peter was petrified. What should he do? If he revealed that he was Spider-Man then Doctor Octopus would know his real identity and Aunt May would be in deadly danger. But if he did nothing then Betty would be taken by this madman. He didn't know what to do.

Doc Ock smiled at Peter, and leapt out of the broken window.

Peter and Jonah rushed to the window and looked down to see him climbing down the side of the building.

'You wanted exciting photos!' yelled Jameson. 'Well, what are you waiting for?'

# CHAPTER 17
# DOCTOR OCTOPUS TRIUMPHANT

In the confusion, Peter ran to the roof of the *Daily Bugle* and quickly changed into his Spider-Man costume. He managed to catch up with Doctor Octopus and followed him across town, making sure that Doctor Octopus couldn't see him. He watched as Octavius climbed in through the window of an apartment near the docks.

When Spider-Man got to the apartment, he climbed up the wall and peered in through the window. He could see Betty and Doc Ock inside. But why were they here? Betty had her face turned away from Octavius and was trying to ignore him.

'So, you don't think Doctor Octopus is good enough for you to talk to, eh?' the mad scientist was saying. 'You cannot ignore me!'

'Sorry, I don't talk to fish,' said Betty.

Spider-Man prepared to burst in through the window. He was nervous because the last time he had fought Doctor Octopus he had been badly beaten. But he had to be brave for Betty – she was counting on him.

Just then a tall man in a blue suit walked through the door.

'Betty!' cried the man. 'What's going on? Octavius, why did you bring my sister to my apartment? Why are you both here?'

Spider-Man realised the man must be Bennet Brant. He waited outside the window, clinging to the wall. He couldn't save Betty unless he knew what was going on, he told himself. But also, part of him was scared.

Inside the apartment, Doctor Octopus grabbed Bennet Brant with two of his mechanical arms and slapped him with his real hand. The slap wasn't hard, because without his robot arms Doctor Otto Octavius wasn't a strong man.

'I'll tell you what's going on!' said Doctor Octopus. 'I'm in charge. Everyone does what I say! You...' He picked up Bennet and dangled him in the air. 'I know that you are a lawyer for Oscorp!'

'What?' said Bennet. 'I don't know what you're talking about.'

'You're the lawyer for Oscorp, my previous employer. You were part of the team that fired me and banned me from entering the laboratories. Now I can no longer continue my work. You will give me access to the Oscorp laboratories and remove everyone else from the building. Tell them they are fired!'

'I will not!' said Bennet.

Peter had to do something, but he was so scared he could barely move. Doctor Octopus was stronger and faster than him. He closed his eyes and jumped through the window, into the apartment.

'Take me to Oscorp and I'll let your sister go!' Doc Ock was shouting.

'That's what I call a *squid pro quo*!' said Spider-Man. Making stupid jokes seemed like a good way to hide how scared he was.

'Leave me alone, you insect!' shouted Doctor Octopus, sending a mechanical arm shooting towards Spider-Man.

'I know, I know, that pun was a bit *fishy*. I'm sorry,' he said, leaping over the arm and ducking another one. A third arm caught him hard in the face, and for a second he saw stars.

Peter could feel that spider-sense in the back of his neck every time the metal arms started to move towards him. It was warning him of the most dangerous angles of attack.

Bennet and Betty ran and hid behind a couch, while Spider-Man and Doctor Octopus were fighting.

The robot arms were twisting and turning as if they had minds of their own, which in a sense they did. The artificial-intelligence chips in each of the arms were allowing them to think and move much faster than any human brain.

'Have you ever thought about getting a more accurate villain name?' said Spider-Man, dodging another arm. 'How about Doctor Creepy-Shouting-Man?'

The apartment was too small for Spider-Man to be able to fight properly. Every time he jumped out of the way to avoid one of the robot arms, he smashed into another piece of furniture. He tried climbing on the ceiling to get a better angle of attack, but Doctor Octopus threw a chair at him which hit him hard in the chest.

Spider-Man fell to the floor, hitting his neck on the table as he went down. 'That is going to hurt in the morning!' he said. But he couldn't stay down, he had to get up and save the Brants.

As he pulled himself to his feet, a robot arm hit him in the nose, then another flipped him off his feet.

Again he tried to get up, and again he was knocked back. This time the robot arms were pummelling him in the stomach like a boxer. Two, three, four, five blows and his abdomen felt like it was on fire. He didn't know how much more of this he could take. His costume was being ripped by the spinning pincers on the ends of the tentacle-arms.

'What are you a doctor of, anyway?' said Spider-Man, wincing through the pain. 'Is it bad haircuts?'

'I happen to like this haircut!' said Doctor Octopus indignantly, but his eyes darted round to check his reflection in the window.

Spider-Man used this distraction as an opportunity. He slid down, ready to strike, but he wasn't fast enough. Two of the arms coiled around his wrists and squeezed. Spider-Man heard the crack of something breaking in his web-shooters, but he was in too much pain to think about it. He tried to wriggle free, but he couldn't. He was stuck.

'Leave him alone, you monster!' shouted Betty, running from behind the couch.

Doctor Octopus raised the tired Spider-Man. 'You're right,' he said. 'This idiot is a waste of my time.' He dropped Spider-Man and picked up Bennet Brant instead.

'I'll do whatever you want,' said Bennet. Doctor Octopus laughed, dangling him higher in the air, then squeezing him. Bennet cried out in pain.

'Time for us to leave, I think,' said Doctor Octavius, and he pulled Bennet out of the window. Spider-Man tried to chase them, but he fell back on the floor. It looked like Bennet's arm was broken.

'Why didn't you stop him?' shouted Betty at Spider-Man. 'Jonah was right about you. You are a menace!'

This was the angriest Peter had ever seen Betty. He couldn't blame her. He had failed her. He had failed everyone.

# CHAPTER 18
# SPIDER-MAN NO MORE?

Even at his worst, Peter had never felt as bad as this before. Doctor Octopus hadn't just beaten him, he had utterly defeated him.

Worst of all, Bennet Brant had been injured. Once again someone was hurt because of Peter's failure.

Spider-Man's costume was in tatters. It was clinging to him like a wet plastic bag, and it felt as if a strong gust of wind might pull the whole thing off. It was still intact enough that nobody could see who he was, but he was fairly sure that a large rip around the back meant Betty could see his underwear.

How embarrassing.

Peter ran to the window without saying anything to Betty. There was nothing he could say to her. As he jumped out of the window, he raised his right hand to fire his web-shooters and...

Nothing happened.

His web-shooters had been crushed in the battle with Doctor Octopus! Now he was falling from the window of Bennet Brant's apartment with no way to stop himself. He tried to fire the web-shooter on his left hand but that one was broken as well.

Spider-Man hit the ground. Hard. He landed on his left shoulder and he felt something give way. He rolled as soon as he hit the ground, but he was in agony.

As Peter trudged his way home, he started to think maybe it was a good thing that his Spider-Man costume had been ruined. Maybe Spider-Man had been a mistake, and it was time to give this all up.

When he got home it was dark, so Peter

climbed up the wall of his house and through his bedroom window. His shoulder burned in pain whenever he pulled himself up with his right arm, but he didn't want Aunt May to see him like this.

Peter Parker took off his ruined Spider-Man costume. His suit was in tatters and his web-shooters were broken. He sighed and threw everything under his bed.

He fell asleep almost immediately and was woken the next morning by Aunt May insisting on driving him to school.

'It will be nice for us to spend some time together,' she said, and Peter couldn't refuse.

When they were in the car, Peter noticed Aunt May was looking pale.

'Is everything OK, Aunt May?' asked Peter.

'I'm fine,' she replied, a little too quickly.

'Are you sure?' pressed Peter.

'Well, there is something, but I didn't want to worry you. It's nothing really,' said Aunt May. 'The doctor decided that I need more tablets for my heart.'

'More medicine?' said Peter. 'Are you OK?'

'I'm fine. I shouldn't have told you anything,' said Aunt May. 'I don't want you to worry.'

'I can try to get some more money to pay for the medicine,' said Peter. 'Let me help.'

'I don't want you getting any more photos of that terrible Spider-Man,' said Aunt May. 'I know what you've been doing. I saw your name in the paper. The *Daily Bugle* is right. He is a menace and I hope that he goes away and never comes back.'

'Maybe you're right, Aunt May,' said Peter, staring out of the car window. 'Maybe Spider-Man should go away.'

Peter was lost in thought for the rest of the day, worried about Aunt May, Betty and Doctor Octopus.

He thought about all the times Aunt May had saved her money so that he could buy new toys or science books. She hardly ever bought new clothes, and she never went out to expensive restaurants. He couldn't remember the last time she had spent money on herself. Peter realised that he had been out a lot being Spider-Man recently, leaving her alone in an empty house.

He was thinking about this at lunch when Liz Allan pushed past him.

'Hey Liz,' said Peter.

She ignored him and kept walking.

'Is something wrong?' asked Peter, wondering why people didn't just tell him when something was wrong.

'It's just that... I thought you were going to ask me to the dance!' said Liz angrily.

The dance! He had completely forgotten about it. The dance was that evening, and with all the Spider-Man drama in his life, it had slipped his mind. Everything in Peter's life seemed to be falling apart because of the time he had spent being Spider-Man.

'I, uh, I was going to ask you,' he said. 'I meant to. I just... I've had a lot of other things going on recently. Are you going to be there tonight?'

'Flash is taking me,' said Liz. She softened a little and smiled at him. 'It would be good to see you there, though.' Then she walked away.

Peter stared after her. What was he supposed to do? Should he run after her? Did Liz like him now? One thing was sure, he was definitely going to the school dance that evening!

Suddenly he felt his spider-sense tingle. Danger! Had Doctor Octopus followed him here? Was Liz in danger too? Was anyone in Peter's life safe?

He whirled around just in time for Flash Thompson – who was jumping to catch a football – to knock into him and send him flying. He hit Peter's injured shoulder, which hurt so much that Peter yelped in pain.

'Oh, Parker, I didn't see you there,' said Flash. Peter couldn't tell if this was true, or if Flash was punishing him for talking to Liz Allan. He wasn't sure which was worse.

'That's OK,' said Peter, as Flash helped

him to his feet. 'Flash, what would you do if Spider-Man gave up being Spider-Man? If he never put his costume on again?'

'Parker, I ought to beat you up for saying that!' said Flash. 'Spidey would never give up. He's too brave! Did you see that online video of him saving that car from being hit by a truck? The guy is the best. He's not a coward like you!'

# CHAPTER 19
## THE BIG DECISION

Betty Brant wasn't returning any of Peter's messages or answering his calls, so he went to see her at the *Daily Bugle*.

'If you're here for my secretary, you're too late!' yelled J. Jonah Jameson as soon as Peter got out of the lift. 'She's visiting her brother in the hospital.'

'Her brother? Is he OK?' asked Peter.

'Well, no. He's in hospital,' barked Jonah. 'But he'll pull through. Doc Ock really hurt him. He's nearly as bad as Spider-Man! I bet the two of them are in cahoots. Do you have any pictures of Spider-Man and Doc

Ock together? Action ones or scary ones, preferably. I want photos that will make people choke on their morning coffee.'

'No, I don't know where Spider-Man is,' said Peter. 'I don't know if I will ever see him again.'

Aunt May was watching television when Peter got home. The first thing he saw on the TV screen was a huge image of Doctor Octopus. The Parkers' television was old and damaged, which meant that everything had a green tint. This made Otto Octavius look even more terrifying than usual.

The news reporter on the television seemed excited.

'*Reports are coming in that Doctor Otto Octavius, also known as Doctor Octopus, has attacked Oscorp Industries. Police officers are unable to enter the building, and—*'

'Oh Peter, please turn that down,' said Aunt May. 'That Doctor Octopus is nearly as bad as Spider-Man!' She looked pale and unhealthy. Peter gently reached over her and picked up the remote. He turned the sound down, but he could still see the grotesque image of Doctor Octopus.

Peter knew that he should stop Doctor Octopus, but he couldn't face putting on the Spider-Man costume right now. Maybe this was the end. He just wanted to go to the school dance and see Liz Allan. If he did try to stop Doctor Octopus, then Jonah would just use it as an excuse to write even worse things about Spider-Man and make people hate him even more. He couldn't win.

Bennet Brant had been hurt. If Spider-Man got involved maybe more people would be hurt.

Peter tried not to think about what Doctor Octopus was doing right now. Doc Ock had beaten Spider-Man before and he would beat Spider-Man again. He could see on the screen that Otto Octavius had taken over the Oscorp laboratories. People were getting hurt.

'Aunt May, have you been taking your

pills?' he asked.

'There are so many pills,' said Aunt May. 'It's a waste of money. I'll be fine.'

She didn't look fine, thought Peter.

'You have to take your pills!' he said, trying not to shout. 'I know that they're expensive, but we will afford them. You need these pills! Without them, you'll...' Peter looked away, not wanting to finish the sentence.

Aunt May leaned over and held his hand. 'I don't want anything getting in the way of your studies,' she said. 'You're going to be a great man, Peter.'

He paused. 'Does being a great man mean always doing the right thing?' he asked. He was looking at the news footage of Doctor Octopus.

'Of course,' said Aunt May.

'Even if you might fail?' said Peter.

'Peter, everyone fails sometimes! That's how we learn things,' said Aunt May. 'If you never fail, then you never grow. I thought that Ben and I had taught you that.'

'I don't know...' said Peter.

'Peter, you have so much potential, so much power in your future,' said Aunt May. 'And remember what Uncle Ben always said? "With great power comes great responsibility".'

'With great power comes great responsibility,' Peter repeated. She was right. That spider bite had given him incredible powers, and whether he liked it or not, they came with a responsibility.

'But promise me one thing, Peter,' said Aunt May. 'Promise me you won't put yourself in any danger. I couldn't bear it if anything happened to you.'

Peter promised, but he was thinking about Doctor Octopus.

Doctor Octopus was hurting innocent people at Oscorp Industries. Someone had to stop him. The police clearly couldn't.

Peter Parker had been given his powers for a reason, and it wasn't to look good or to be popular. It was to save people who needed saving. He had failed in the past, but that didn't matter. He was going to try again, and keep trying, even if it meant missing the school dance and disappointing the one person at school who was nice to him.

Peter ran upstairs and pulled his ruined Spider-Man costume out from under his bed.

## CHAPTER 20
# SHOWDOWN!

It took Peter more than an hour to fix
his costume. The arms had been almost
completely ripped up by Doctor Octopus's
pincers, so he needed to rebuild them
from scratch. He used padding from an old
Halloween outfit to reinforce his costume in
the places where it was shredded. He knew
these were the places Doc Ock was going to
hit him the hardest.

His shoulder still ached, but the rest of his
injuries were starting to heal. He bandaged
up his shoulder and hoped for the best.

The web-shooters were crushed and

twisted, but not completely broken. He could see how the pressure mechanism that opened the nozzle to fire the webs was blocked. Uncle Ben would've known exactly how to fix it.

Carefully, Peter bent the web-shooters back into place, then replaced the main lines that fed the web fluid to the nozzles. But they still didn't work. Eventually he fixed them with some baking equipment taken from Aunt May. He upgraded them so that he could adjust the amount of webbing he used.

Finally he created a new, extra-special batch of web-fluid. Now he was ready.

'Doc Ock, I'm coming for you!' he said.

He climbed out of his window and swung out into the night. He looked out to the distance in the direction of Midtown High. People would be arriving for the school dance about now.

He sighed and swung off in the other direction, towards Doctor Octopus.

When Peter arrived at Oscorp Industries,

there was a ring of police officers and police cars all around the building. Blue and red lights reflected in the large, dark windows of Oscorp. The building was in darkness, except for a single light on the top floor.

Spider-Man perched on the top of a lamp post, looking down at the NYPD and considering his next move.

'Hey! What are you doing up there?' shouted one of the police officers.

'Uh, I'm here to fight the Octopus guy,' said Spider-Man. 'You know him? Brown hair, wraparound glasses, likes to scream a lot. Has four metal arms?'

'Get down here!' ordered the police officer. He was a tall man with a thin moustache and an angry look in his eye. 'You're that Spider-Man freak, aren't you?'

'Always nice to meet a fan,' replied Spider-Man, jumping down from the lamp post. 'I'm assuming you're here because you want an autograph?'

'Arrest him, officer!' yelled J. Jonah

Jameson, suddenly appearing from behind a police van. 'Quick, Eddie, get a photo of Spider-Man being arrested!' A large man appeared, holding an expensive-looking camera. He scowled at Spider-Man and took his photo.

Great. Now Jonah would make Spider-Man look like a bad guy *and* Peter wouldn't even get any money from the photographs!

'Jonah? What are you doing here?' asked Spider-Man.

'The press has a right to be here, you masked maniac,' yelled Jameson. 'Brock, why aren't you taking photos of Spider-Man being arrested? Officer, why aren't you arresting him? Do I have to tell everyone how to do their jobs?'

More police officers were running towards Spider-Man. 'Get down!' yelled one of them. 'Get down now!'

'Is this like a disco "Get down" thing? Like "Get down to the funky beat"?' he asked. He jumped up onto a lamp post, flipped to land on another lamp post, then did a little dance.

'PUT YOUR FEET ON THE GROUND, RIGHT NOW!' screamed a female police officer.

The police were between Spider-Man and Oscorp. There was no way of getting to Doctor Octopus without going through them.

'Look, we both want the same thing,' he said. 'We both want to stop Doctor Octopus. Let me through and I can help!'

'Don't trust him! He's probably working with Doctor Octopus!' shouted J. Jonah Jameson.

'I can do... things that you can't!' said Spider-Man. 'I have these powers. You've seen me! I'm your only chance at stopping him. Have you seen what he can do with those arms?'

Two of the police officers nodded sheepishly. 'We couldn't get anywhere near him,' one of them admitted. 'He was too fast for us. We didn't stand a chance.'

'I could take on Doc Ock!' said another

officer confidently.

'Sure thing, Steve. You go first,' said the first officer.

Steve didn't move.

'I want to help,' insisted Spider-Man.
'You're just a guy in a mask,' said the female officer. 'Put your hands behind your head and sit down on the ground!'

Peter could feel his spider-sense prickling on the back of his neck. He was in danger.

He jumped over the officers, landing neatly on a police car. Before anyone could react, he was up again, flipping in mid-air and bouncing gracefully off a police van, then a wall, then another police car.

He was close to the entrance of Oscorp Industries now.

He could hear Jonah yelling 'Get him! GET HIM!' at the top of his voice, and officers were running, but he was too fast for them to catch him

He ducked away from one officer, then jumped twelve feet straight up in the air to avoid another.

*THWIP! THWIP! THWIP!* Spider-Man used his new adjustable web-shooters to web three officers' feet to the ground.

Then, with one last jump, he was there! He sailed through an open window, waving goodbye to the police officers outside.

He was inside.

'Pizza delivery!' he yelled out. 'Order for Doctor Octopus?'

A mechanical arm reached out from the darkness and grabbed him, pulling Spider-Man into the Oscorp laboratories.

# CHAPTER 21
# SPIDER VERSUS OCTOPUS

As soon as Spider-Man entered Oscorp Labs, he was punched in the face several times.

'Why did you come here?' screamed Doctor Octopus. 'I told the police to leave me alone! Why are you trying to sabotage my work?'

'Because your work was incredibly dangerous last time and it looks even worse now?' replied Spider-Man while deftly blocking a punch.

Spider-Man realised that he needed to shift the fight to somewhere where he was more comfortable. He jumped up and stuck to the ceiling to give himself a moment to breathe.

The Oscorp building was dark. Doctor Octopus had turned all the lights off, which meant that everything felt dangerous and unnerving. Peter realised that Otto Octavius had been wearing shades the last two times he had seen him; maybe his accident had affected his eyes somehow?

'This ends now, Doctor Octopus,' said Spider-Man. 'We can either do this the easy way... or the punchy way. It's up to you.'

Octavius had clearly been working on something big. Scientific equipment was spread out all over the laboratory. Peter could recognise a linear accelerator and a Geiger counter, which he knew was used to detect radiation.

If he scuttled quickly enough around the ceiling, he could evade Doc Ock's whirling arms. Spidey feinted right, then jumped left. He launched himself at Doctor Octopus, fists first, pushing forwards with all his might.

Peter punched Doctor Octopus hard in

the face, knocking him to the floor. Doctor Octopus screamed and grabbed him with a robot arm, throwing him across the room. Spider-Man couldn't stop now. He needed to keep up the attack.

'Not so funny when you're the one being punched in the face, is it?' said Spider-Man.

The next time he jumped, Doctor Octopus was ready and swatted him away like a fly. Spider-Man crashed into a table of glass beakers and test tubes, sending broken glass flying all around him.

'Ooooh, were those expensive?' said Spider-Man. 'You know what, just take it out of my wages at the end of the shift.'

Again he jumped and again he was knocked back to the floor. He hit his shoulder and for a moment it was so painful that he couldn't speak.

'You can never defeat me!' crowed Doctor Octopus.

Spider-Man took a deep breath then stood up. He was NOT going to give up, no matter

what. This wasn't working. Doctor Octopus
had beaten him twice before, and if he didn't
change things up, Octavius was going to beat
him again. He needed a new plan.

'Don't go anywhere – stick around,' he
said, firing his web-shooter and sticking
Doctor Octopus's feet to the floor.

Then he ran out of the main laboratory
and into the corridor. Maybe there would be
something around here that could help him.
He ran past conference rooms and branching
corridors until he suddenly stopped in front
of a sign on a door that said *DANGER:
CHEMICAL STORAGE!*

The door was locked. He ripped it from
its hinges and looked inside the room. 'I can
work with this,' he said to himself. These
chlorides and acids were the same chemicals
he had used for his science project with
Uncle Ben.

Spider-Man had an idea, but he had to
act quickly, before Doc Ock found him.
He got to work, mixing chemicals. When

he was finished he stuck his camera to the ceiling – if he was going to do something this dangerous then he wanted to make sure he got photos.

Ten minutes later, Doctor Octopus burst around the corner. 'I've got you now!' he shouted.

'I'm not scared of you – you have Slinkys for arms!' cried Spider-Man.

Spider-Man was holding a lasso made of webbing. Inside the lasso were five glass test tubes, filled with a light-blue liquid. He spun it over his head.

'Here! Catch!' he shouted, throwing the lasso towards Doctor Octopus.

Instinctively, two of Doctor Octopus's robot arms reached up to grab the lasso and the test tubes as they flew towards him.

The test tubes broke with a crash, covering his mechanical arms with the blue liquid.

'You fool,' laughed Doctor Octopus. 'My titanium steel arms are far too strong to be damaged by acid. You've wasted your time!'

'Doc!' said Spider-Man. 'Who said I was trying to hurt your little friends? I don't know why you're being so cold to me.'

Doctor Octopus realised too late that the chemical Spider-Man had thrown at him wasn't an acid, it was an adhesive. Spider-Man had just stuck two of his arms together! The arms wriggled and thrashed, but the mixture Spider-Man had created was too strong. They were stuck.

'I don't need all my arms to defeat you!' snarled Doc Ock.

'Are you sure about that?' said Spider-Man.

Now it was time for part two of his plan. Spidey reached behind his back and grabbed the flashlight he had taken from the storeroom. He shined the light directly into Doc Ock's eyes.

Doctor Octopus screamed and turned away, his remaining robot arms flailing wildly. This was Spider-Man's opportunity.

He leapt forwards, punching Doctor Octopus, again and again. The robot arms tried to grab him, but they were much more easy to evade now.

'One, two, three, four...' Spider-Man counted the punches as he hit Doctor Octopus. 'Five, six, seven, eight, nine... that's ten tickles from me! Ten tickles, tentacles – get it? Wow, this is good stuff and it's wasted on you!'

A robot arm shot out and smashed into an X-ray machine. Something inside the machine sparked, and flames shot out of it.

Spider-Man didn't even notice. He was too busy fighting Doctor Octopus. His shoulder felt like it was on fire, but that didn't matter, he couldn't stop now. He was so exhausted that he could barely stand up, but if he stopped fighting he knew it would be the end of him.

Spidey summoned up all his strength for one last punch. This was it.

*WHAM!*

Spider-Man felt the vibration of the punch through his whole body. He started to fall to his knees. He had nothing left in him.

Doctor Octopus was still standing...

Then he fell back, unconscious. Spider-Man had defeated him!

He was about to celebrate, when he realised he was weirdly hot. He looked around. The lab was on fire. Everything was on fire.

Doctor Octopus was passed out at his feet. What was he going to do?

# CHAPTER 22
## A
## NEW DAWN

The easy thing would be to leave Doctor Octopus and run. The man had tried to kill him. But Peter Parker could still hear the words of his Uncle Ben: *with great power comes great responsibility*. Spider-Man had incredible, amazing, spectacular powers, but those powers came with a price. He had to use them in the right way.

It felt like every muscle in his body was fighting to make him lie down and go to sleep. Arms aching, he reached down, picked up Doctor Octopus and hoisted him over his shoulder.

Slowly, step by agonising step, Spider-Man carried Doctor Octopus out of the burning building. Coloured flames burst from barrels of chemicals while sparks flew from different machines, but he didn't stop and he didn't he put down his enemy.

Finally, he kicked open the main doors of Oscorp Industries. The police officers had been joined by firefighters, but nobody was going into the building. Spider-Man dropped the unconscious body of Doctor Octopus at their feet.

'Did... did somebody order the fried calamari?' he said.

Before any of the stunned officers could respond, Spider-Man fired his web-shooters and swung off into the night.

The next morning, the *Daily Bugle* called Spider-Man 'the worst criminal the world has ever seen', but Peter didn't care. He even smiled at the part where Jonah had written that the fire at Oscorp Industries 'may have been started by Spider-Man's webs (or possibly loose wiring)'.

He had begun to realise that not everyone was going to like Spider-Man, and that was OK. It was more important that he do the right thing than be liked.

Peter had left his camera stuck to the ceiling taking photos of the fight, and Jonah paid him a lot of money for the photos of his fight with Doctor Octopus. Enough money to buy Aunt May's medicine for a long time.

Peter messaged Betty Brant the next day and asked her if she wanted to go for coffee. He was feeling more confident, and he enjoyed spending time with Betty.

'How is your brother?' Peter asked her when they met.

'He's getting better,' said Betty. 'I know that Spider-Man helped catch Doctor Octopus, but I still blame him for what happened with Bennet. You take photos of him. Do you think you could help the police catch him?'

Peter realised that Betty was only

interested in him because of his links to Spider-Man.

The next day during Science class Peter made sure he sat next to Liz Allan.

'I'm sorry... about the dance,' he said to her. Liz didn't reply at first, so he kept talking. 'I've been trying to work out who I am and what's important to me. I made some bad choices. I'm sorry.'

Liz smiled at him.

'Thank you, Peter,' she said. 'I know you've been through a lot over the last few months.'

'Yeah,' said Peter. 'It hasn't been easy.'

'Have you talked to anyone about your uncle?' asked Liz.

'I mean, my Aunt May,' said Peter. 'But it's hard to talk to her because she's going through a hard time too...'

'Why don't you tell me a bit about what he was like?' said Liz.

Peter told her about Uncle Ben's favourite things: about how he loved wrestling and helping Peter with science experiments and working on his car. Afterwards Peter felt a bit better.

That night Spider-Man swung through Manhattan.

As he swung past Central Park, he saw a hooded man trying to grab a businessman's briefcase. Spider-Man swung down feet-first, kicking the robber and knocking him to the ground before he could run away.

A small crowd saw what happened and started clapping and cheering.

'Thank you so much!' said the businessman.

'You go, Spidey!' shouted another man in a leather jacket.

Peter Parker looked around at the smiling, clapping people and didn't know what to say. People were cheering his name and slapping him on the back. He felt fantastic, like the whole world was on his side.

As Spider-Man swung away he caught sight of his own reflection in the window of

a skyscraper and realised that he was a hero.
He would make mistakes sometimes, but that
was OK. He was trying as hard as he could
to help other people.

He was making a difference.

He was Spider-Man.

# CHAPTER 1
# DISASTER IN THE ARCTIC

'Girl, are you *seeing* this?'

Over the phone, Spider-Woman's voice
somehow managed to sound both horrified
and just a tiny bit excited, which was
actually pretty standard for Captain Marvel's
friend.

Carol – Captain Marvel – stared at the
video footage on her TV screen.

'Yeah,' she said. 'I'm seeing it.'

Something extremely bad was happening
in the Arctic. The news programme was
showing live footage of what looked like
a volcano erupting from deep beneath a

glacier. The ice was quaking with the force of a thousand bombs going off all at once, as something ripped its way up from far below the surface. Massive cracks began to appear in the ice, tearing jagged chunks out of the snow-covered landscape.

'There are people there,' said Spider-Woman. 'Look!'

The shaky footage was showing a ship caught amid the freezing waters, being thrown this way and that in the choppy ocean. As Captain Marvel watched, a huge cliff of ice sheared off from the quaking edge of the glacier and crashed into the water, sending an even larger wave towards the struggling ship.

'Have you got this?' asked Spider-Woman. 'I'm kind of tied up right now. You know I'd be there if I could, right? I'm not just leaving you to do this on your own because I hate the cold. I mean, I *do* hate the cold – snow, ugh, yadda yadda yadda – but that's beside the point.'

Carol grinned. 'Chill. Put your feet up. Have a snow cone.'

'Funny. You're just so *funny*, Carol, that's what I like about you.'

'Can't chat, stuff to do,' Captain Marvel told her friend, as she ran towards the open window of her apartment. 'I got this. Catch you later, Jess!'

She tossed her phone onto the couch and leapt up to her window ledge, pausing for a split second before throwing herself out the window.

The wind hit Carol in the face as she launched herself into the air, her heart beating a crazy rhythm in her chest. It didn't matter how many times she did this, flying just never grew old. How could it? She was flying! It was just the best feeling to be out here, to be free of gravity, to be free of everything, soaring away from the ground and into the sky.

Captain Marvel left New York City and North America behind, rising higher and higher until the edge of the continent curved away from her. She headed north, flying as fast as she could. She had to find a way to stop what was happening before the ice cap collapsed completely. But first, she had to save the people on that ship.

As she reached the ship, Captain Marvel could see that it was in real trouble. It was simply too small to navigate the huge waves crashing into it. Massive chunks of the glacier kept breaking off, plunging into the ocean and sending yet more water washing over the bucking ship. It made Carol think about what would happen if the whole ice cap melted – cities all over the world would suffer a similar fate.

She could see people on the ship's deck desperately clinging to whatever they could. It was going to sink if she couldn't save it, and quickly.

'You're the strongest woman in the world,' Captain Marvel reminded herself. 'You can do this.'

Carol shot towards the ship faster than a bullet from a gun. She hovered at the ship's prow, just above the icy water, feeling it splash against her suit as she found her grip.

Then she began to lift. The effort made her muscles burn, but the ship began to rise out of the waves, saltwater streaming from the hull. As another gigantic wave burst across her back, Captain Marvel gasped. Still, she didn't let go.

Second by second she gained momentum, shoving the ship clear of the waves until she could set it down on smoother waters again. She let it go and hovered above the deck, letting the water trickle off her suit.

The people on the deck of the ship started to notice her. They looked like the crew of a research vessel – these weren't seasoned deep-sea sailors. Were they scientists? Then Carol saw the logo on their jackets. It belonged to a global oil company.

She turned to look at the disaster still happening beneath the ice, then back at the people below her.

'Hey,' she said. 'Do you know what that is? Do you know what's happening out there?'

One of the men struggled to his feet, his face pale.

'We – we didn't know,' he stammered. 'We didn't know this would happen!'

Captain Marvel landed on deck, standing before him with her hands on her hips. 'You didn't know what would happen? What did you do?'

'We found something beneath the ice,' the man said. 'It must have been there for centuries, but with climate change, the ice has now melted enough for us to detect it.'

'What is it?' Carol demanded. 'What did you find?'

'We don't know. Some sort of machine. We thought – *I* thought – that if we could get it out, we might be able to use it to mine the oil that's below the surface. But something activated it before we could get it out.'

'Now it's destroying the entire ice cap,'

said a women next to him. 'If that happens, these waves are going to look like droplets in comparison with what will come next. It will destroy *everything*. Earth will never be the same.'

'Not if I can stop it,' said the super hero. 'Get out of here. Get the ship as far away as you can. I'll deal with this – whatever it is.'

Captain Marvel flew into the air again, speeding back towards the rupturing mass of land and ice. A shape was visible now, a dark shadow was forcing its way towards the surface from beneath the splintering ice and snow.

Something punched its way free of the ice. It was a massive metal hand. It smashed down into the snow, clutching for grip as it hauled itself free of its icy prison.

'It's a robot,' Captain Marvel said aloud. 'It's a giant metal robot! Why is it *always* robots?'

# CHAPTER 2
# A MIDNIGHT ADVENTURE

Sometime after midnight on a cold, clear night, the silver-and-red toy robot that Carol had just got for her fifth birthday decided to wake her up and start talking.

*'Robot Supreme to Carol Squirt Danvers,'* it said, in a low voice that sounded a lot like her big brother Stevie. *'Directive from Robot Control says: Wake up! You're missing all the fun!'*

Carol blinked her bleary eyes and stared at the robot. It had snuck under the duvet she had pulled up over her head.

'What?' she asked.

'*Not "what?"*,' the robot corrected her primly. '*Sorry!*'

Carol blinked again. 'Sorry, what?'

'Never mind,' said Stevie in a hushed voice, appearing from the side of the bed and dropping the robot on her pillow. 'Just wake up!'

Carol Danvers' childhood home was in a quiet suburb of Boston, where she lived with her mum Marie, her dad Joe and her two stepbrothers, Stevie and Joe Junior. Though her brothers were a few years older than her, they never minded their little sister hanging around with them. Like now, for instance, when Stevie had snuck into her room to wake her up to play, when she really should have been fast asleep.

'What's happening?' Carol mumbled, still sleepy.

'Ssh,' Stevie whispered. 'Come on, Squirt, we're going on an adventure.'

To five-year-old Carol, the idea of an adventure in the middle of the night was both exciting and scary. She sat up and rubbed her eyes. 'An adventure? Where? Are Mom and Dad coming?'

'Nope, it's just us and Joe. You'd better hurry, or you'll miss it. Put on the warmest sweater and socks you've got.'

'Are we going very far?' Carol asked.

'Yes,' Stevie said. 'We're going into space. Hurry up!'

Carol rushed to do as her brother said and then followed him out of her room and down the hallway, treading on tiptoe past their parents' bedroom.

She held her breath as they crept down the stairs, avoiding the one that always creaked. Once they were downstairs, she looked around for her other brother.

'Where's Joe?'

'He's already started the adventure,' Stevie told her. 'We're late!'

Stevie took Carol's coat from the hook in the hallway and made her put it on, as he quietly opened the door. Then they went out into the garden. At first Carol couldn't see anything because it was so dark.

'Can't we use a flashlight?' she asked.

'No!' Stevie told her. 'There need to be as few lights as possible or your eyes won't adjust. Come on.'

He led Carol further into the garden.

'Hey, Squirt,' said a voice near Carol's left foot. 'You made it, then.'

It was her brother Joe. He was lying on his back on the grass, zipped inside a sleeping bag. There were two other sleeping bags laid out beside him.

'Quick, get in,' Stevie told her, as he sat down and began to get into his own bag.

Carol did as she was told. 'I thought you said we were going into space?' she asked, disappointed that they hadn't gone any further than their own backyard. She'd imagined a beautiful silver rocket carrying them up into the night sky.

'We are,' Stevie told her. 'Lie back and look at the stars.'

She did. Carol had never really paid attention to the stars properly before. The more she stared into the darkness, the more pinpricks of light she could see. They were never-ending, and there was so much to take in that her eyes could barely manage it.

Joe's watch started beeping, a tiny sound muffled by all his layers of clothing.

'Okay,' her brother said, as he turned off the alarm. 'Showtime, people.'

'Watch really, really carefully,' Stevie whispered to Carol. 'You'll see something moving. It's going to come over the top of the house.'

All three of them were silent, but Carol didn't know what she was looking for.

'There!' said Joe. 'There it is!'

'I can't see it,' Carol cried. 'What does it look like?'

'Ssh,' Stevie said. 'Look again. It's a light, and it'll be moving.'

'A shooting star?'

'No, slower than that. Look carefully.'

Carol squinted. Then she saw it! A bright light, just like a star, but it was moving through the night sky in an arc, right over their house.

'What is it?' she asked in wonder.

'It's the International Space Station,' Joe told her. 'You can't always see it from Boston, but tonight you can, just for as long as it takes to travel through our sky.'

Stevie nudged her. 'There are six astronauts up there right now, Squirt,' he said.

Carol watched the little light that was the ISS sail steadily over their heads. She tried to imagine what it would be like to be one of the astronauts inside. How would it feel to be out there, among all those stars, in space?

They watched the light move until it disappeared from view. Then they watched the stars a little longer.

'Right,' Stevie said after a while. 'We'd better get you back to bed, or we'll all be in trouble in the morning.'

Carol didn't move. She was too busy studying the stars.

Stevie nudged her again. 'Squirt?' he asked, as Joe unzipped his sleeping bag and stood up. 'You fallen asleep?'

'No,' Carol told him, still looking up at the stars. 'Just thinking.'

'Oh? About what?'

'I'm going to go up there one day. I'm going to go to space.'

Her brothers both laughed, though Carol didn't think they were being mean.

'Good for you,' said Joe. 'Our little sister, the astronaut.'

* * *

The next day, Carol asked her mum to take her to the local library.

'I want to learn about space,' she said, over breakfast.

Her dad stopped eating his oatmeal. Her mum and dad shared a look that Carol didn't understand.

'Please, Mommy. If I'm going to be an astronaut, I need to know all about the stars.'

'You don't want to be an astronaut, honey,' said her dad. 'It's dangerous.'

'I do,' Carol said, stoutly.

'You could be an engineer instead,' her mum pointed out. 'You could build space shuttles. That would be cool, wouldn't it?'

'I want to be an astronaut,' Carol insisted.

'It can't hurt to look at some books, can it?' Carol's mum said to her dad.

He sighed. 'Well, if you think it's a good idea...'

They went to the local library and asked the librarian for books about space. The librarian seemed pleased to be asked and pulled out several volumes for Carol to borrow.

'Is this for a school project?' The woman asked.

Carol shook her head. 'No. I'm going to be an astronaut.'

The librarian grinned. 'That's a wonderful

goal to have. Did you know that before you can be an astronaut, you need to know how to fly an aircraft? That's why one of the main routes into the astronaut programme is to join the air force.'

'Oh,' said Carol. 'Then I guess I need to learn to fly.'

The librarian smiled and pulled a thick tome from a higher shelf.

'This is meant for adults really, but I think it'll be perfect for you. It's about one of my heroes. Her name is Helen Cobb. She's a pilot and she's broken all sorts of records. This is a book about her by a journalist called Tracey Burke. She followed Cobb around for a year, writing about her. I think you'll love it. It's got a lot of great photographs, too.'

Carol took the book – it was big and heavy – and looked at the cover. It showed a photograph of a smiling woman standing in front of a beautiful silver plane.

The plane reminded Carol of the rocket

she'd imagined bursting out of their backyard.

She didn't hear anything else the librarian or her mum said that afternoon – she was too busy looking at photographs of her new hero.

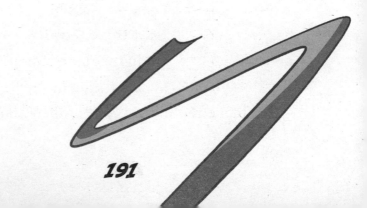